Rabbit Stories

Rabbit Stories

by

Kim Shuck

Poetic Matrix Press

ISBN: 978-0-9852883-8-9

Poetic Matrix Press

www.poeticmatrix.com

Dedications always run the risk of sounding like an award acceptance speech and this one might. This writing, as with all of my writing, is for my family: all of the usual suspects and for Etta Mae Rowe, my great grandma; for all of the people who've collected me as kin over the years; for various rabbits: Tim, Martin, Leo, John, Doug, Graham and Dominic. In particular this is for my kids: Morgan, Ed and finally for Bee, sleep well baby.

Rabbit and Rabbit Food
Cover Art by Michael Horse,

Most people who have seen ledger art painting are familiar with the work done from the middle of the 1800s until roughly the 1920s in the Northern Plains. I'm assured by Michael Horse, the cover artist, that there is ledger art from many places and even many countries. It's an artform that is enjoying a renewed popularity and there are a number of active ledger artists showing some very exciting work. The form, drawings on pieces of 'waste' paper, has been shifted in the work of Horse. He generally chooses an image that enhances the content of the background writing. In the case of our cover he's chosen paper with the commodities food records from a town in Oklahoma, where part of my family is from. I don't know what Michael was trying to say with that, but for me it says that our stories feed us one way and possibly better than the white flour, canned meat and lard that replaced our traditional diets.

Kim

Drawings by Scott Smith

Scott's mother says that she could take him anywhere if there was a pencil so that he could draw. He was a delightful child. Smith went to the School of the Museum of Fine Arts, Boston and then returned to rural New Hampshire where he enjoys drawing in his sketchbooks with his daughters.

Kim

Contents

Transformations

Legends

About the Author

Preface

Rabbit is a trickster in Cherokee stories. He makes wagers, he talks his way out of being eaten and he is generally an unreliable being. I've always had a soft spot for him. He is thought to be an inspiration for the Brer Rabbit stories. It's also been said that the Cherokee got him from other South Eastern traditions which may or may not be true. I can't really say as I wasn't there when we started telling about Rabbit. Cherokee Rabbit isn't the only long-eared trickster. Loki is said to have transformed himself into a black rabbit when he was doing some mischief, the Anishinabe tell stories about their own great rabbit. There are bunny tracks all over the place.

These stories are not old rabbit stories, these are my rabbit stories. This isn't a book of anthropology, it's a book of fiction. If you attribute moral content to any of the moments I describe, that content is purely your own. I take no responsibility for chewed book covers, dust tricksters or stolen girlfriends. Guard your cilantro.

Kim

Rabbit Stories

Investigations

Rabbit and Quantum Theory

If you put a quantum scientist in a box and never open it again will anyone ever understand the uncertainty principle? What does the uncertainty principle have in common with Native American philosophy? If I do not set foot on the scale between mid-November and mid-January did my weight actually spike in December? Why does anything care if I measure it?

I see Rabbit. He is weighing and measuring leaves so that they can exist, so that he can effect their existence with his regard. We are all in community, the subatomic particles wait for Rabbit's gaze so that they can dance in the music he makes by looking. He takes this responsibility very seriously, making sure to look at them during auspicious and ceremonial times. Rabbit is careful with the subatomic particles. The ground does not have the ability, after all, to support his weight unless he takes the next step. He is careful not to think about the Ukten while he is looking at the particles. Instead he whispers, "beautiful, happy" he cradles them in his sight and they dance.

It is difficult to find either the scientist willing to be boxed for the sake of theory or the box that would contain her. She is busy after all, measuring her own corner of the cosmos. Not, I hasten to reassure you, putting mustard seeds into stolen skulls. She is watching the dance... well, that and doing laundry. Even quantum scientists can't avoid the laundry. That experiment insists upon being measured. It is like the old-time water clocks: time will stop if there is no laundry to drip from drawer to bin, a brief moment on the skin in-between. She knows that she has a variety of measuring tools available. Pleasure in the feel of clean cotton on skin, although difficult to get funded, is certainly one of her tools.

Rabbit spends his weekend being a rabbit. He munches contraband cilantro, intended for the family quesadillas and contemplates overlaps between theoretical physics and Green Corn ceremony. It is important to take responsibilities seriously, he munches in a rabbity way. Later he will sprawl floppily, he has chosen to be a lop this weekend, enjoys the softness of this form, its acuity of taste. Things like to be thanked so he plans an experiment of thanks, decides to conduct it in the spring rather than the fall. There is enough silliness about thankfulness in the fall already, thinks Rabbit.

At the pow wow people dance. Circle the arena. As men and women look at each other in all combinations, they dance to the music of the looking, to the music of being looked at. This weekend no one drops any feathers.

Rabbit makes sure to measure himself in the mirror every day. Quantum self-definition, he thinks. Pinching an inch of extra waistline, he smiles to himself, evidence of good stew past. He exposes his teeth, sucks thoughtfully, considering things to chew. Soon he will go back to the pow wow to look and look and look and whisper things to the people as he looks, "beautiful, happy". He cradles them all in his sight and they dance dance dance dance.

The quantum physicist, her grandma and a collection of Aunties sit at the kitchen table. A large rabbit has claimed space under the table, where the physicist used to sit with her crayons and her magnets and her collection of small empty bottles. A suspicious smell of cilantro wafts up towards her. She listens to the Aunties as they talk of stew, the making of stew, the dishing up of stew and the relative merits of various root vegetables. The physicist ponders all possible meanings of the word 'relative'. A munching sound from below provides counterpoint. She has been promoted to the space above the table... wonders if this means she is becoming an Auntie. Maybe Rabbit has the right idea, remaining below.

There is a wild rose that the people call Rabbit Food. Rabbit licks his lips at the thought. Beauty thy name is Rabbit Food. He imagines a vine trailing up a paw paw. The tree is heavy with fruit. He has thought about every leaf, every blossom and naturally every bit of fruit. Rabbit sighs and looks at the legs of beautiful women, of women who discuss food. He knows their names, these women... and one is named for that rose. Rabbit Food is talking about stew, about potatoes, about spicebush... and especially about bean bread. She is more beautiful than he remembers her, even though he thinks of each of her cells singing happily every day. He thinks about the beautiful lines he is singing around her eyes, they are not finished yet, but they are a song of smiling.

She has been plagued by Rabbit all of her life. How could she not have been? What had they been thinking with that name? Now there was no cilantro in the fridge... and she thinks that a certain tubby lop might well be to blame. Ah well. It is time to gather the clothes in from the line. She feels that small closed boxes are suspect, even those that dry the laundry. Besides, there is such riot of plant life to cradle the wash in happy thoughts. She doesn't know all of them, but they smell like happy thoughts. Such song and dance for the creek underground at the foot of the garden, this is so good for the subatomic particles in the laundry. No telling what the effect might be on that experiment. The experiment would have to run its course.

There is a certain wildness to this garden. Rabbit finds a damp and shady spot and greedily eyes the berries to be. He makes promises of undying love to the berry canes. Truly, what could be more undying than being together forever... and he intends to eat them up, to add their songs to his, to become the box and the contained, and to sing them in his cells for all time.

She spreads sheets crisp with the songs of plum tree, of apple blossom, of milkweed and of Rabbit. With so many military folk in the family she knows the right way to tuck in sheets. You can bounce a quarter off of a bed that she makes, no mistake.

Rabbit becomes both softer and more clever in this garden. He watches the striped spider weave. She rarely has time for him, he learned long ago not to disturb her weavings. He blinks warily at the memory. Spider, serious as she is, enjoys Rabbit's company, but the only clue is her slightly more formal posture. She weaves intently. Measuring everything carefully she creates her web, her blanket.

The physicist had saved the quilt for last. The sheets are for the military men in the family; the quilts... well the quilts she'd learned about from the Grandmothers. She spreads this quilt gently. It is soft from love and use, soft from thoughts and experiments. Each piece of the quilt is its own thing. The quantum physicist settles her inheritance onto the bed and goes off to stir stew.

Rabbit Food visits
the Place of Pigeons

The anthropologist shivers in the back garden. November in London and she doesn't know enough stories from this place to keep her warm. Some neighbors are trying to get her to speed but it's cold cold cold here and no amount of walking Regent's Canal, not to the River Lea or to Camden Lock, seems to be helping yet. It is raining in a way that Londoners would not call rain and the horse chestnut tree fills with Magpies.

Robin Hood/Fox/Rabbit watch her from their burrow at the foot of the garden. To be honest, it isn't a large garden so they have a very good view. Her hands cradle a mug of fir tip tea. He has always loved her hands. The steam rises according to an equation that both she and the tricksters know. She is out of context and it is making Robin dizzy, making him be more things than even his complexity can encompass. He isn't usually both Rabbit and Fox. He slips more completely into Robin Hood and contemplates the confusion inherent in an unfamiliar form of multi-culturalism. Then he looks again at the arcane angle of Rose/Rabbit Food's eyes and thinks that it just might be worth it.

Mudhens are intently doing mudhen things. Rabbit Food walks next to her man down Regent's Canal. The regent in question, one of the most trivialized characters in the history of the monarchy, was notorious for gambling, women and debt. He was also responsible for this canal, a beautiful park and other urban improvements in London. As always, the mistress wins out in column inches. Barges are intently doing barge things. Some move up or down the canal: locks filling and draining. Some nose through the Islington tunnel, an aqua incognita. Its side tunnels and nooks occupied by the small urban spirits of inconvenience: the imp of signal failure, the efreet of off-key busking, the minor demon of splashed puddles. Something darker, larger, lazes there in that tunnel, something that St. George didn't kill. Increasingly it amuses itself by closing the Blackwall Tunnel and tangling traffic. Mostly it sleeps and listens to the stories of London: stories in layers, stories of clay becoming brick, of fires singing clay to hardness, of water licking brick back to clay, of dissolving statues. She hears the thing stir, can feel it wondering about them. If this were North Carolina, if the thing were the Ukten, they would be dead already. Britain isn't the Smokies, similar isn't same. She trusts her guide to keep her safe. Her tall man buys a cone of chips and a fishcake. He makes an offering of one chip to a guardian mallard and the very large, very old thing in the tunnel rolls over sleepily and dreams of Bishop Bonner.

Fox/Rabbit/Robin Hood begin to like this man of Rabbit Food's, though Robin likes him least of the three. He licks his brown/red muzzle and considers a mallard supper. No one else wants duck it seems, so Fox trails the couple through an unfamiliar sunlight. Ah well, he has become an urban fox, and isn't as sure of his hunting, but there would be good eating after the trash bins were put out. Rabbit shudders a bit at the thought. Robin fingers an arrow. The tunnel thing, old as old makes them all a bit nervous, particularly when it dreams of murderers, even governmentally sanctioned ones, particularly this close to November 5 and Bonfire Night. The other two contemplate Fox for a moment. 'No relation,' he assures them. They are not convinced.

Still walking the canal, and water is doing water things, creating mud, dissolving stone, half hiding both old and new things. As the heat of Autumn drains to Winter the blaze of leaves fades to a muddy foxfur beige and they fall, the colors of shredded brickwork, into the canal. Rabbit Food and her man pass another lock, fallen leaves are kicked into a tan, brown and black flame under the water by the rising levels. Along the canal factory buildings in reuse or disuse blink at them through empty window frames or full ones. Boarded buildings subside, are subjected to the prying of bramble and nettle. A cure for fever grows between loose paving stones that ring as they step on them. Rabbit Food is as lost as she can be when she's so hemmed in by tale spinning. The continual crawl of it, half heard as mumble, makes her feel a little ill. Her man squeezes her hand and begins to talk story to her. London, city of words, starts to warm.

Rabbit/Robin/Fox feels her headache begin before she does. This connection is awkward in both directions sometimes. Though she does remember to drop a periodic chip for him. Chips are not cilantro, they are not carrot or lettuce or Rabbit Food, but chips have their own charm. Rabbit is practical after all. Rabbit Food/Rose's man has a low voice. He winds out tradition after history about street names, poems of navigation, tales of purpose. He is a quiet talent, that one. They would have to watch him.

She watches as they light the pyre. It's raining, but it IS London, it IS November. There had been wine, a sparkling white that we must not call champagne, and then a red. There had been salad, rich with dried tomato and olive. There had been fresh tomatoes dusted with black pepper, there had been a bowl of citrus fruit. Now they were going to enjoy the fire that gave the holiday its name. This would be a fire with no effigy, no Guy twisting in recurring immolation. The anthropologist's people understand a controlled burn. She hears the canal barely ten yards away, smells the rain — a sycamore. These wild English folk move around the ceremonial fire: one begins to roast chestnuts. Earlier, in the park there were fireworks, the math of them taming the flames — making the emotions safe. London, city of clay and stone and words — ok, and water — sings a centuries-old passion for burning — like Rabbit/Robin/Fox/Guy. London of the canals, London of brick, calls its fears, warms its hands at the fire, roasts chestnuts.

Robin watches the man as he feeds Rose a chestnut. Rabbit hopes that he drops one. Fox hopes that the fire spooks something small into flight. Robin thinks that he doesn't like Chestnut Man — he looks like a forester. Rabbit laughs at Robin's possessiveness, 'She doesn't belong to any of us, not even to me.' Just then Rose sneaks a chestnut into her left hand and tosses it towards Rabbit who catches it neatly. 'Not that we don't have an understanding.' He happily munches the perfectly roasted nut. Robin shakes his head in disbelief even as he tastes the coveted treat. This polyvalent reality was beginning to feel like a personality disorder, and the ears and tail had to go. 'What does she see in him anyway?' He glares at the tall, broad shouldered man who is shelling another steaming nut. 'Cute accent,' Rabbit says around another mouthful. Rabbit and Fox both burst into laughter.

Spellcasting

Rabbit Food watches her Grandmother weave thread around her fingers. Her hands make shapes like the mudras of statues in the museum in the park. She doesn't know mudras, or what they mean yet, just that they have something to do with thread and her Grandmother and something called tatting. She isn't brilliant at it right away, but she works hard. In the back of her mind it is always about bronze statues, women draped in yards of jewels and little else, the faint smell of peanut butter cookie dough. She is in second grade when she closes her first circle, knots lining up on the string in the same direction as dancing; the direction of dancing things into balance. The bunny, as familiar as thread — as familiar as the stuffed musical tiger on her bed, he watches with a total stillness. It doesn't occur to her to mention him to anyone. She feeds him a cookie and keeps learning the things she needs. Four or five rings fit easily. It is possible to make six and three fit well. Two or seven spring 3-D.

Rabbit loves presents. He loves this little girl's curiosity song. There is both a patience and impatience to her that makes him smile. She is saved from prettiness by eyes that challenge everything. He spends hours just watching her work it all out. He doesn't know this game with knots and string but it focuses her and makes her lovely. He sings about knots and the cleverness of careful fingers.

Sometimes it is hooks, sometimes needles or a needle but it is always the thread and what she can coax it to do. There are endless bookmarks, hair ties, fabric with images embroidered on them. Rabbit Food is chased through all of them by small, crisp peanut butter cookies cooling on a torn brown paper bag. Sometimes she puts the thread down long enough to help roll teaspoon-sized balls, to smash them with a sugared milk glass, to mark their surface with a fork in a pattern that might be a basket start. It is never long before she is back to the thread: twisting, coaxing, knotting. She becomes strange with books and threads, has to investigate the elder women down the street when her Gran's knowledge of thread is exhausted. Hairpin lace, drawn work, everything but sewing: she follows the thread through the maze. It is always the thread.

For Rabbit it is the cookie-crumb trail. He is generally bored by now but this devotee of spider makes sure to leave him cookies, thinks strange shapes. He wants to see what it will be next and so sings curiosity, geometries from all corners of Rabbitdom. He doesn't push. He watches.

Rabbit Food tracks the grass dancer, regalia thick with yarn. He has come to the arena first. He coaxes down the grass in the school gym so that everyone can come out and dance. The grass, the yarn and the dancer suggest shapes: irregular solids, arabesque arches and repeating curves. Women's shawls trail like koi through the ponds at the tea garden. Traditionals' feathers, comment fog and thread. Like a Mexican wedding dance, knotting something with their toes. Lions tumble acrobatically, the fan moves in the woman's hands, the bamboo pole beats time on the floor. In the museum the statues' hands make careful shapes. All ink in Pacific ocean water, a song of Rabbit Food's study of thread.

Jasmine hovers at the base of Rabbit's tongue, then a salty rice cracker wrapped in nori. He lets his eyes unfocus as Rabbit Food ties quipu, scholar's cords; layered interpretations of song knots scroll though cruschiki, bigosh, golubki, squash soup, broadswords and fried catfish. He reclines. 'Oh but this child makes me work hard'. This tugging and untangling, this shaking the whole of the web of it all. Nearly silent Spider laughter follows him and he can't tell if the taste in his mouth is threads of tea or incense or the rubber bands she uses to make a toy. Unremembered calendars, love poems and spells for safety fall from her fingers and are collected in boxes of family memory with pictures from each school year: posed, out of context images that will never make real sense again. Rabbit is dizzy and stays dizzy. Rabbit cannot look away.

Rabbit Food's father watches her as they sit in the hippy café. Her cocoa cools in its cup, whipped cream looses its connections and subsides. She's tying knots again. He smokes and watches. Threads of smoke rising, threads of cocoa drying in ridges on ceramic substrate. Knots on thread. Cotton is expensive; costs land, people, time. Rabbit Food loops and sings and dances. "Who taught you that?"

"Gran." Gran denies this, lays out an embroidered cloth. Rabbit Food ties knots in string. Rabbit Food dances.

The Historian Heads to a Medieval Church

Rabbit Food is making pow wow cookies. Don't look them up; this is a very regional behavior, the locus of which is Rabbit Food's kitchen. Like the traditional yuletide lobster cookies, pow wow cookies — if they occur in multiple locations — are the product of convergent evolution and not an example of connections between populations. Pow wow cookies generally take one of two forms: spicy peanut butter chocolate chip or black cocoa, white chip and dried cranberry. They travel to the pow wow in a red tin. The red tin is in San Francisco. The peanut butter/chocolate chip cookies are in London. Rabbit Food sighs and looks around.

Rabbit is very very happy. Fox sits with his nose straight up in the air. Robin looks for a way to steal a cookie. 'Theft is not necessary,' Rabbit shares. 'She always makes a few especially for us.' Robin likes stealing, and so continues to look for an opportunity. Fox continues to fill himself with the smell   of spicy peanut butter and chocolate. Rabbit sings age-old songs of happiness and deliciousness to the cooling cookies. He knows that there is no pow wow, he'd have heard if there was going to be a pow wow, but cookies were welcome either way.

The smell of her baking sneaks up the stairs and rummages at Chestnut Man. Rabbit Food feels his confusion. She hears him draw his robe from the door's hook. His feet on the stairs are a woman's cloth dance drumbeat in her arches.

She hits the kettle switch before he gets to the turn in the banister, throws a PG Tips sachet into a mug from some cold war bunker turned tourist destination and turns in time to watch him spin around the banister post.

'Is she going to give us a biscuit or not?' Robin is grumpy. Fox nips at him in correction. Rabbit ignores him; he watches the woman with pleasure. He had sung those smile lines around her eyes and mouth himself, and it was good when she showed them. Her baking was better when she was happy. The smell of spice and chocolate and peanut is a breathable mood. 'When I bother with work,' Rabbit thinks, 'I'm damn good.' A slim and lightly furred arm threads up between the stove and the counter top, selects a blemished cookie that had been set aside, and slips back under the stove. All three of the jesters watch. 'That's interesting,' observes Robin. They all stare in unison.

Rabbit Food is anxious. She feels the overwhelming flood of stress words sneak into her mouth. 'Vicar, vicar,' she repeats to herself, 'not father, vicar.' Like all historians – she loves churches. Loves the paperwork of them, the layers of building, the little carved things, the graffiti and the stained glass, the spiders in the corners. Rabbit Food, like many grown into multi-religious families, hates church services. She is anxious about unfamiliar dialog and choreography. Today's event will reportedly be social. Rabbit Food is not convinced. Rabbit Food knows small towns, and small towns know Rabbit Food. The cookies are, like her stress words, too flashy for the event. She can't help herself. Conspicuous is not good. On the other hand, there is no way to be inconspicuous. If she wasn't American, if she didn't have dangerous, nearly yellow eyes, if her breasts weren't heavily obvious, if she wasn't arriving with the quiet and quirky local prodigal, she would still not be from this small Essex town. She will wear her blue jeans, the gauzy white shirt with the black tank top under it; she will pull on the cowboy boots over the variegated socks she knitted herself. She will wear one of the four pieces of good Ndn jewelry she'd brought with her, three of them made by her. She will do this for Chestnut Man, even though he doesn't want to go either. Rabbit Food is going to be a spectacle, but she was named to be a spectacle – had turned it into an art form. She smiles at Chestnut Man, gives him a cookie to have with his tea, repeats to herself: 'Vicar, vicar, vicar, vicar.'

Rabbit doesn't spend much time on this island, mostly only to visit the bones of a former project. Boxes in the British Museum were one thing; long animate arms from beneath the stove were another. Fox and Rabbit look at Robin who shrugs, 'No one I know.' He nods at Chestnut Man. 'That one may be Viking tall but he smells of Essex flint and dawn rain. I'm originally from Birmingham, not the South East. That,' indicating the stove with his chin, 'that could be almost anything... except a brownie. It's too big for a brownie, and it's older than I am.'

Chestnut Man and Rabbit Food pack the car. There really is no tin for the cookies so they are arranged on a plate and swathed in clingfilm. Rain falls, quiet love words, persistent and soothing. They look at each other, touch. He starts the car and heads for the M11. Road works punctuate. They pass a theme park with a petting zoo and a large water tower painted like a Holstein. She feels herself becoming a mythical creature: skin sprouting feathers, pupils changing. Rabbit Food is strange even to herself here. She strokes the beads of her bracelet: black, blue and red. A gift, the student's first major work, it contains all the insights of new things. She feels the feathers smoothing away. Chestnut Man wonders if she is getting car sick. 'Not exactly,' she assures him. He asks that she let him know. She nods.

No one is thinking about the arm from under the stove. The shift from London to Essex is a body shock for both Fox and Rabbit. Rabbit in particular cannot get right with himself. Do semi-deities get car sick? 'Too many stories too fast,' chokes Rabbit. 'The plane was high enough, this is torture.' Battles, holy wells, house fires, burrows dug; stories rolled by at 80 in the fast lane. Fox just keeps wanting to run run run, and Chestnut Man runs them, pulling Rabbit Food, Fox and Rabbit along with Robin in a headlong dash to church no less frenetic that that of 800 CE. Robin eyes the cars they pass, evaluates the drivers net worth. He knows that Chestnut Man won't stop, but this road, this pathway into Essex, this is   exactly his kind of place. He strokes an arrow shaft and waits.

Eventually the traffic thins. They shift onto smaller roads near Stansted airport. Across over and down they roll through the first old town: the book bindery, the fancy pub and the Rolls dealership. Rabbit Food looks at Chestnut Man quizzically. 'Folks moving up from London,' he observes. Her mouth twitches with amusement. Some of the houses are thatched here, thatching cut in decorative patterns. The roads softly rock Rabbit Food, soothing her until they come to the crest of another hill. She can see the church spire from there. The building commands the area from the top of its own hill. The church is huge; if Chestnut Man hadn't said 'church' she would have thought 'cathedral'. The rest of the town is overshadowed, a collection of slouching houses far too old for formalities like right angles. Down another dip and up the church hill, they pass houses with name plaques, little village businesses and one place labeled 'Dick Turpin House'. As the event looms, Rabbit Food has one more moment of dysphoria and then she relaxes.

Rabbit crouches on the floor of the car gagging silently. Fox chokes down his own panic: this is exactly the kind of area where fox hunts would have happened, were they still legal. Robin is looking out the window with interest. 'Dick Turpin,' he said in an undertone. 'We were butchers here I think.' Rabbit wrinkles his nose.

'Wasn't Dick Turpin real?'

Robin turns to Rabbit and looks at him heavily, more powerful than Rabbit had ever seen him, 'We're all real.'

Growing a Biologist

Rabbit Food waters the tomato plants, the pepper plants. She lets her two-year-old 'wallow the bean-beans.' His face is very serious as he gives each plant exactly the same drink, squatting in that boneless way that toddlers have, pouring from the watering can. The dirt hisses like kettles, like gators. It's going to be hot. The orange tomatoes — the ones they planted in the old cut-down wine barrels — glow like coals, like persimmons. She picks a soft one and shares it with the boy, bite for bite. They trim, dig, garden. Crazy dogfight dogs from next-door keep up commentary. The street cat watches over them — doesn't trust those dogs for anything. The boy finds the spring at the foot of the garden, finds the salamanders that cluster there, finds the jawbone of a rat. He shows her the bone on a flat and careful baby hand, doesn't touch the living animals. He wants to know what they are, wants to know everything.

Rabbit thinks that the boy is an interesting addition to Rabbit Food, but he likes the lemon pound cake she's taken to baking even better. This boy is not Rabbit-curious, but he's respectful and Rabbit appreciates that. Rabbit snuggles into a hollow in the dirt. The cat dismisses him. They both track the dogs. Not their fault, the man over there beats them, beats them until they'll fight — weapon dogs, self-ambulatory guns, an assertion of masculinity. They growl and bark and

bark and bark. Rabbit chews the last mouthful of glorious
tomato and watches them.

Rabbit Food and the boy sit on the front stairs in the sun
and read. The nervous, black, not-her-dog dog has avoided
them both since she tried shaking the boy. Rabbit Food
doesn't even remember picking the dog up to illustrate
shaking, but she has it on good authority that that's exactly
what she did. The boy is quiet as she reads to him; large
brown eyes examine her face intently. Naming him for his
Grandfathers has made him serious, quiet. He likes dragons,
dinosaurs and gators — begs to be taken to the aquarium
over and over, watches the octopus tease her lunch and
shakes his head. She's too smart to be locked up in a small
tank and they all three of them know it. 'Bored things get
mean,' the boy says.

Rabbit doesn't like the wet and hates the aquarium. He
has recurring nightmares of drowning in water that teems
with gar. Even the sad and solitary manatee frightens him in
spite of his flotilla of lettuce. He is a small furry thing in a
building full of the finned and scaled. Rabbit tries to be even
more clandestine than usual. Rabbit Food's boy likes the
same route every time: past the bones, the stuffed ibex and
buffalo, past the pendulum and the pocket watch collection,
around to the gators. Rabbit really, really doesn't like the
gators. The room is hothouse humid and his ears sag.
Droplets form on his bunny lashes. Rabbit is miserable
at the aquarium.

The boy needs to look at each snake. He needs to find all
of the ones that hide. He needs to identify individual
characteristics of the toads and frogs. He leaves the spiders
alone. He loves the hot wet air of the place, has a soft spot for

these seemingly dispassionate creatures. He especially loves the one that bangs its nose on the glass. That one should be let go. He wonders why they aren't in systems rather than isolated. His sturdy body in a stance of anger, every cell raging when a random man hits the glass and the upset snake tries to strike. Rabbit Food soothes him. They leave the aquarium, wander in the park, feed ducks, feed squirrels. She shows him how to sit in the moon-viewing garden, carefully holding a nut. He curbs his excited trembling as a grey squirrel timidly approaches. He is still. The squirrel — tail a propeller — comes closer and closer until it snatches the peanut and runs off up the tree. The boy explodes into excited laughter. Rabbit Food spins him. She bends over and ties a spell into his laces. They walk.

Rabbit feels a bit left out. She takes the creature everywhere — teaches him things that Rabbit taught her. She encourages his stillness. Shows him things that huddle under stones in the garden. Tells him what day and under what moon greens or sage or spicebush should be planted. Shows him not to gather mint while the plant is blooming. These secrets that were theirs, she shares them with the boy. His eyes are the same nearly yellow concentric tree pattern as hers; they crinkle in the same way. Rabbit finds himself turning flips for him in the night to make him giggle. The boy's fingers are careful on rabbit fur. If he stays it will be all right with Rabbit.

The boy is sick. His face drains, mostly from his nose, but somewhat from his eyes. He looks persistently out the window and sulks. Rabbit Food twines string around her fingers and begins the story. There is malice, she is destroyed — flies into a thousand thousand mosquitoes. The story plays out in crossed threads. She tells him about the man whose bed broke, and shows him with the string. She talks story until the boy sleeps. The next day Rabbit Food is sick. The boy sneaks into her room and watches her sleep. She wakes to his wide, serious eyes. He tells her a story about butterfly dragons. They live in hives and eat bananas and pollen. They send a turtle emissary to negotiate pollen prices with the bees. He strokes her hair. He sings.

The Criminologist Studies Piano

An upright piano stares Rabbit Food down; dark wood carved with roses. The basement room is cold and her fingers move slowly over the keys. Two of the ivory key covers are missing and she orients herself by feeling for them, finds east with her fingertips. Old French Song, which she oddly always remembers in German translation, ponderously unfolds after half an hour of finger exercises. Her Gran stomps on the floor upstairs. Rabbit Food sighs, closes the piano and heads up. The corgi mutt follows her eagerly on the stairs.

Rabbit can smell the bear claws even if Rabbit Food cannot. He smiles. She's never been able to eat two, and he knows that he's faster than the dog. Da da da da da dum... Rabbit sways to the music. Love is food — in this family as in his calculus — and is in abundant supply. Bear claws, cinnamon toast, little jam-filled hard candies with fancy cars on the wrappers. The flavor of a Rolls Royce is raspberry. Rabbit dances.

Gran never wants Rabbit Food to play as long as she thinks she should. There are always cocoa and games of Gin Rummy in the breakfast nook. Strange wallpaper — baskets and fruit picked out in a mustard yellow — the vague memory of Grandpa carefully matching the images, his muscles standing out under the blue-green blur of an old tattoo like a permanent bruise. There are books to read, tucked into corners near heater vents with more cocoa. Warm, it's all warm and food and their need to care for her. Now and forever her Grandpa the only one allowed to call her 'Rosie'. Finally there is Yatzee, and this they all play together – 'Tell your Grandmother it's her turn', 'Tell the old man it's his.' A warm dog drapes herself across Rabbit Food's feet. This is love, this world of cocoa and family games and the smell of dog.

The dog glares in heterochromatic ire. Rabbit needs to be careful. The dog doesn't try to chase, but she is always visibly worried about him. Rabbit is careful, not threatening, and he doesn't run. It's the one blue/white eye that worries him. He knew a wolf like that once – possibly the one that Rabbit Food's clan was named for – memories are thankfully fugitive. He is happy as long as they don't sit in the dining room for their games. Who puts a paint-by-numbers Last Supper over the formal table? This nook is still nearly kitchen – kitchen is food, food is love – and there is no conflicted imagery in this room.

Lawrence Welk is on the console TV. Her Gran and Grandpa sway, still managing not to speak. The few words they do say are in Polish and as furtive as Grandpa's initial steps. Rabbit Food is assured that they were once the best dancers at the Polish club. 'They used to clear the floor,' her Gran says – no reason to disbelieve. Grandpa's handwriting a waltz also, formal and European. Both he and it know their places. This dance is something else. They are the perfect size for one another, short, thick and matched like bookends or the salt and pepper shakers in the dish cupboard. They are careful in most things. Gran still has a washboard. She saves margarine tubs. She has a tool for fixing a run in a stocking. Grandpa has every hand-cranked drill, every saw and every screwdriver he ever used in a career of housing contracting stored carefully downstairs. They even save on words. This dance is something else. Rabbit Food watches them spend all of it in dance.

Rabbit is upside down under the white couch. His mouth hangs open as he watches. These are not part of his family, these short thick... he gazes at his tummy. Well, they aren't his side of the family anyway. His side are outlaws and tricksters: mixed-blood bank robbers, coach robbers and twirlers of rope. These serious people, these savers of blue chip stamps, these careful house renovators; these folk are secret outlaws of their own kind. Rabbit peeks at them from under the couch. He thumps his foot in awe and sings to their dance. They spin, two atoms of oxygen, and do not hear him.

Rabbit Food learns to play piano for these careful people who love her with pastry and card games. She learns to play waltz tunes to their memories — waltz tunes on a carved piano in the basement with cold fingers. She copies the embroideries that Grandpa used to pick out on his white leather trousers in a mountain village thousands of miles and decades distant. He remembers falling asleep to the sound of a floor loom and she learns to play that too, but not before he leaves them. She dreams him taking the dog out. Her strange eyes turned up to him, his hesitant, stiff step as he shuffles out the front door. She comes back to be with Gran then. Reclaims a years-unused room upstairs that smells of leather chair and desk blotter and careful, careful handwriting. She finds a Virgin of Czestehowa medal in the desk drawer and wears it with her small leather bag of other things. She plays waltzes and eventually learns to play the floor loom. Every time she plays them she can see him dancing. Gran makes her a cup of cocoa.

Rabbit re-remembers something about stereotypes that he will re-forget soon enough. He sprawls under the plum tree in September collecting fruit made of this angled Autumn light. Rummages under the tree that Rabbit Food's Grandfather planted when she was born. Practical people these, he gluts on sunwarm fruit: careful set-aside fruit. He gluts on September, small yellow plums. He sings Tatra mountain songs that he must have learned somewhere and thumps his foot. Often he doesn't remember if Rabbit Food or her Gran or her Grandpa are born yet, but he sings to that dance and watches them spin together. Watches the O2 in the air and sings sings sings outlaw songs.

Re-Orient

The Navigator and her dad pack up the car: a box of cigarettes, a flat of pop. Rain starts as they head out across the Bay Bridge. They don't talk. They chase the storm east. In Nevada it sets the world on fire. They drive through the red/yellow/black night. Rainstorm, firestorm — everything tossed. They stop on the freeway with other cars, they all watch for a moment. The bushes burn; howling like the voice of a god she doesn't know. She and her dad not speaking. She clutches the map, it's too dark to read it, but this is her responsibility and she carries it.

Rabbit breathes their smoke through California and Nevada. If these are prayers he can't figure them out. Their silence is boring and he writhes like a two-year-old in church. He knows these roads, these stories. Rabbit Food's silences are difficult for him. In this car she isn't curious, isn't interested. She smokes and drinks pop, her stillnesses almost absorb sound. He is worried. Most of the night it's Utah, salt and salt and freeway and cigarette smoke. Rabbit wants to scream, wants to shake all of the pop cans, wants to run back and forth across the freeway. Rabbit wants to call his fears, to hold them close; anything to interrupt this concentrated quiet.

Morning Red and they are still. They both step out of the car at the next filling station. A redtail patrols the... is it prairie yet? Rabbit Food sighs. Her mouth is dry from the cigs and sugar. They head for Little America. They head for breakfast. Ultimately they head for her father's childhood; to marsh and fishing, to his own heroic dad. They smoke, they drive. They run east, they chase the storm.

Rabbit picks at the French Toast, pours liberal amounts of boysenberry, blueberry, strawberry and fake maple syrups. He slides mutinously around on red vinyl seating, claws making small squeaking noises. He chews the peel off of the garnish orange slice and picks the rest of it apart, scattering bits of orange rubble around on the floor. Rabbit used to live in places like this; places that sell postcards of the Jackalope, postcards of Native kitsch, postcards with recently concocted legends. Roads are the perfect place to attract drama, to cause correctable damage. Just now, with the prospect of another day thick with no words and smoke he is fractious, lonely for fog and peanut butter cookies and books and heater vents. Lonely for her to get active, to take part.

Rabbit Food is a bit nauseous from fake scrambled eggs and salty cubed ham. Her body is stiff from overlong incarceration in the car. She is nauseous from silence. She wants to tie knots but the smoke on her hands makes them feel strange and she can't catch the spirit of it. The storm enfolds them, rocks the car. They are dry, warm and silent – flinging themselves through the rain in the Toyota. She opens the map for the thousandth time, no stars, no sextant, no stories; there are only green road signs a thread of freeway and rain and the map. Near Medicine Bow there is a break in the weather – color drips through the sky. She can't escape the taste of caramel color, of tobacco. They can't outrun the storm and they can't stop. They turn right towards Denver and the storm begins again.

Rabbit has tried every trick he knows. No amount of negotiation with the Thunders, no offering of copious smoke, nothing is helping. She is numb and she isn't interesting when she is numb. He's worried. There is generally nothing quiet about her. Even her thoughts are still. She has become ill and small. Her father also, here in this grey confine of the car. Owl and Cougar, Pine and Cedar, they all keep watch but Rabbit can't sleep even so. He softly sings creativity, affection and joy returning. Nothing sticks. She is closed doors and chemical buffers.

Kansas isn't so much flat as it is gently wavy. They run through it mostly in the dark. The headlights barely show the road. There are infrequent clusters of lights like the stars they still can't see. They follow the thread, the road, the storm. They follow it through the maze of not talking – finding communion or not. They are both stubborn, something she may have from him. Once when she was new he stuck her in a cardboard box and strapped her onto the seat of the MG, drove her somewhere, but she forgets where. It could have been the beach that time. They didn't speak then either, now it's her fault too. The car shudders through the Kansas dark, shudders towards S. Gladys. They smoke, they drink pop, they follow the thread, the storm, the road.

Rabbit's eyes are sticky. His voice cracks. He still sings, falling on his heart as always. He sings and sings, low tones rattling in the dry of his feelings. He can almost feel a way in, isn't sure. The watchers smooth his worried fur, they reassure, they soothe. Finally Rabbit sleeps.

Near Treece the air begins to smell of marsh and acid – of fishing trips and snakes. They've run out of cigarettes and pop, but they are nearly there, nearly home? Hard to know what to call it. Her father changes into someone — almost the boy who ran off to the lake — almost the 17-year-old who ran off to the Navy. Hard to be needed in a place you've left. He shapeshifts there in the car into something he doesn't recognize and Rabbit Food tries not to watch, but the car is small and flooded with two days of silence. She listens as his bones crack, as fur sprouts, his teeth grow, his ears lengthen. She watches out the window as they come up on chat piles.

Rabbit almost wakes to find that things have changed. Something about water, something about breakfast. He peeks out the car window to find the weather indecently clear. No one will believe that it cleared up just now. He shakes his head, it isn't the way the story should go. This isn't how home should be. Here in Ottowa county: semi-dry, Klan ridden, scattered liberally with descendants of the Seven Fires. This isn't right. He rubs his forehead with one hind paw. This isn't the story I was singing.

It's not a smell you forget, this combination of old mine and wet. Here at the center of the maze they cross the bridge where the giant cottonmouth died, they pull past the house with the dogs. She can see the pecan tree, the dead Osage orange, dummy and the cats. It's all gravel and heat. They sit in the car until her Grandmother comes out to welcome them. There will be salted beer, cribbage. There will be the smell of Skin so Soft. They wait for it in the dregs of their drive. Her dad is nearly done changing for now. They wait.

Allegiances

Rabbit and the Joy
of Minor Sucesses

Morning of fog and candles. Fog, not in those wisps but in real, solid mouthfuls. Brick walls of fog arguing against neighbors, against vision. Rabbit Food floats a fruit-scented candle in the bathtub, a whole different way of going to water. The candle, a gift from Chestnut Man, reminds her of wanting to live in an apple tree. Maybe living in her apple tree... well Merlin pulled it off. She releases yesterday with both hands, lets her eyes half lid. There is beading to do, there is cleaning to do, there is laundry; when isn't there laundry? The chocolate cookies with violet extract are cooling on the tray in the kitchen. Rabbit Food sinks, lets her hair flow out, madwoman hair under the water. Rabbit Food washes; candle bobbing on the surface of the water. She is snug in her water, under her fire, closed into her bathroom. She would have loved to know the decision that had tiled this room in blue and pink. Maybe she would change it to brown and dark rose, maybe she would paint the ceiling dark brown, maybe she would paint gold stars there. Rabbit Food untangles her hair with her fingers; she watches the candle flame.

Rabbit sneaks into the neighbor's yard. The cats there like to cause trouble. Rabbit doesn't want trouble, he wants lemons. The Meyer lemon bush is bent under the weight of ripe fruit even in February. He wants something sour, something to cut the fog. This garden is over-organized.

Daffodils and lemons here, the first red bush flower there. Succulents are tucked in by the fence. Rabbit tries to be patient. He moves from behind a concrete pedestal to behind the fall of jasmine. No cats yet. He moves from jasmine to bare fruit tree. He moves from fruit tree to under the lemon. He steals four lemons, one rind slightly chewed by snails, but heavy, promising juice. Rabbit makes a break for the back stairs. A low growl from under the magnolia makes him run faster. Something flies over him, taking the black shape to the grass, the two shapes roll to a stop near the plum tree. The boy's old man cat, grey with thinning fur, had interceded with the neighbor cat. He waited, posed, like all old fighters. The neighbor cat growled. Grey cat waited, still. The neighbor cat huffed, then cut and ran. Grey cat washed a paw as if it were just any day. Rabbit juggled the lemons up the stairs and into the house. He hadn't realized that the cat would defend him. Grey cat ignored him in a deliberate way, earning a rabbit giggle.

Somerset of rainbows, of swathes of grass, of light rain; Somerset unwinds before them. They drive into the sunrise, light wringing color from raindrops. Thirteen rainbows from London to Bristol, two sets of doubles; this is crossing a country? California or even Oklahoma are a longer ride. This is no headlong assignment of panic, this is a visit. West, an unlucky direction, but this time it's beautiful, liquid, trees and rain. Rabbit Food avidly explores the map, names she doesn't know, names she only knows in reuse. They stop, find take-out tea and sandwiches. They go, heading again towards Bristol. Bristol, perhaps unfair that all she knows about it is the slave trade. There are wars that never end, that only grow lazy. Rabbit Food imagines something like what she's been seeing: patchwork of buildings, new/old some subsiding, some repurposed. The songs of grey and beige and brick trail up and down streets named for horses, for saints, for murderers. She imagines chained people dragged from ships, and shakes that thought away. They have a task, a visit, an offering to   deliver. Chestnut Man isn't much for dropping in on family. He is the child who ran: Holland, Africa, the United States. Now he is both home and not home. He is London and Essex. He is this trip to Bristol. Rabbit Food wrings from him stories about trips to Bath. He thinks out loud about visiting his sister, maybe having lunch. Bristol is confusing streets and bad signage. Bristol is cobbled-together buildings that speak of its own experience of the Blitz. Bristol is an enormous cathedral and getting lost over and over even with a map. Rabbit Food is happy enough to leave.

Robin loves motorway travel and always has. This road doesn't have enough cover, but road nonetheless. Fox is sleeping. Rabbit is counting rainbows and figuring out what is different between this place and his home. Robin snorts. Motorway cafes are not coaching inns. There is a bookstore, there is a Marks and Spencer. Imported fruit, sad salad and bottled water are stacked in neat displays. The bookstore is just bizarre: cookbooks, gardening books and novels. Who reads in a car? It would make sense in a railway station, but car travel is more direct, more intimate. The bathrooms are hilarious, particularly the vending machines. Wet wipes, condoms and sexual lube are on offer for a few coins each. He wonders briefly what plain-flavored lubricant must taste like.

Rabbit Food stands in the sea cave, eyes smarting from salt spray. Waves ring the cliffside like a bell, every seventh wave slopping onto the walkway and making the tourists shriek. She makes a wish for the new year and scatters tobacco. Outside light barely greens the water at midtide.

High tide would fill the cave, low tide would reveal sand and
more light. She walks through to the baths side of the tunnel,
probably access for the old railway at some point. The pools
lay revealed, stagnating salt water is dotted with gulls. Bits of
blue/green tiling cling to some of the fouled pool edges. She
knows that if she kicks the brown dirt she can bring up glass
slumped from the fire that took the place down in the 60s. It
had been a marvel, had filled the valley next to the Cliffhouse.
Higher on the hill there had been the mansion, though that
may have been a bit of an exaggeration. These remnant bits of
robber baron folly had fired her imagination as a child. It had
changed since then, had been made safer, tamer. Footpaths
had been paved. They'd replanted native flora, including the
lavender flowered thing that smelled like nothing so much as
slightly sweaty foot. Rabbit Food watched as fools climbed
out to the fishing rock. Bodies washed from there wound up
in Santa Cruz, hours down the coast, and could generally only
be identified by dental records. Perhaps that would make a
better sign than the slightly vanilla "Dangerous Waves" that
was bolted to the stone there. Rabbit Food heads up towards
the diner and a hot cup of tea. Idiots would generally be
idiots, and would not be told.

   Rabbit frolics in spite of the hawk overhead. He rolls in
pungent plants, he chases sparrows, he finds a scrap of blue
tile. Rabbit is silly with sea spray, with light wind, with the
smells of unpopular plants. Cypress lean away from the wind
farther up the hill. Rabbit, being Rabbit, leans into it, lets it
whip his ears.

Remnants

Rabbit Food stares at Belle Starr's piano. Har-Ber
Village is in Grove, there on Grand Lake, and is a giant
antique museum. She is exploring the music building, finds
this   piano. She wonders what May liked to play, if she
enjoyed   finger exercises. Her own fingers twitch, part of her
would love to coax sound from the old instrument: stroking
the keys, time travel. The woman had been family, Rabbit
Food couldn't remember how except that it was through the
Starr men May had married. She had an overwhelming
sensation of nearness: they had close birthdays, had both
been taught to play piano, they shared locations. She
wondered if she could find out what sheet music had been in
the piano bench, wondered if Myra/May/Belle had been
distracted by bunnies and bunny energy, wondered who had
shot her. Some relative would know, Frank probably. Maybe
she could have him take her to Robber's Cave and tell her
tales there; no crimes are ever unsolved. Someone always
knows. There is an underlying silence for Rabbit Food in
Oklahoma -- both related and   unrelated to the general lack
of city sounds. Cicadas bagpipe constantly, maddeningly.
Pecans, berries, the patchwork of family stories: all voices
chanting in what is almost a map of that red earth place. Still,
there is a silence to it all: a fisherman's waiting, Cotton and
Ot's Xmas tree fish crèche, the long swimming strokes of a
alligator snapper the size of a washtub and Belle's quiet

piano. Come early to water, use the correct bait and every story there is will take the hook.

Rabbit lets her wander the museum. He can make his own fun here. He resets all of the clocks so that they show different times. The dogwoods and redbuds are far more reliable anyhow. Rabbit takes a wander though Annie's garden, across the flowered lawn. He nibbles this and that, visits things friends had stolen, things friends had brought with them from Europe, the East or from Cherokee. Objects of self-definition or of re-invention swirl around him. Rabbit rolls a cigarette and prays at the water's edge. He prays and then starts rolling vanilla flavored dough balls. Rabbit smiles, time to go fishing.

Rabbit Food was after some laundry on the first bright day in about a month. She breathes deep, the lichen is exhaling in the cool shadow of the house. Amazing scent surrounds her. She does a turn around the garden, bruising rosemary, nutmeg geranium and pineapple sage. She checks the currant bushes, small white flowers dotting the canes promised sour, red berries. The blue ginger plant was larger and still showed no sign of ever blooming. The few remaining bulbs were poking up. Significantly there was one lone blossom on the plum tree. Last year's tomato bushes were dry and brittle in the January wind, one or two red fruits clung there yet. Soon there would be new plants, the tree would be snowy, then full of sweet, yellow plums the size of cherries. Rabbit Food sprinkles tobacco where the stream would be if it were not piped under. She rests a hand on her apple tree, the one her Gramps had planted at her birth.

Rabbit curls into a fork in the apple tree. All rabbits should be able to climb trees. He sighs, looks downhill at the amazing view. Gardens are growing things, but they are not wild. Rabbit is missing the wild, missing warm rain and the Smokies. He doesn't miss his foggy hills often, but when he does... Rabbit finds a fugitive apple from last year, holds it between his front paws and tastes summer past. His eyes half close in pleasure. Rabbit shivers, listens for the stream underground. Rabbit listens for the E flat minor of the water he sings, the water that pushes red through his veins.

Rabbit Food's hand throbs. She can barely move, is curled in her sleeping bag. She watches the vibrations trail from the bug wings, trails in astounding colors. Susan waves the mosquitoes off of her face, retrieves some chocolate ice cream and feeds her spoon by spoon. Her arm feels like melted cheese, like a strummed rubber band. Rabbit Food giggles. Susan feeds her water. They'd been picking blackberries earlier, the scrapes run up and down her arms, twine around them like snakes. Ruby stains streak from her fingertips to her elbows, marks glowing in the half-dark. She boils in her skin, she tosses. Susan gives her ice, tells her stories. Rabbit Food can't say thank you, she can barely swallow the water. She and Susan are camp friends, don't see each other in real life, but Susan is the real deal at camp. They'd been in nursery school together, their friendship marked by playing dress up, the smell of the cornmeal box and the musty pillows in the reading pit of the quiet room. Susan waves away the bugs. Susan brings her more ice.

Rabbit and the pine trees keep watch through the night. The girl's ten-year-old body glows more brightly than ever,

glows red. The pine trees shush his fretting. The long cool
fingers of her friend stroke the girl's face, they offer ice-cream,
they offer ice. Her body is strong, whatever it is she fights. She
fights like a creature born for fighting, like something from a
world of battle. Rabbit suffers, so many gone like that:
twisting and sweating. The pines shush his fretting. It's the
1970s not the 1800s; she is strong, she fights. Rabbit stirs
water, he rolls a cigarette, he breathes on a transparent stone.
Snakes of poison wrap her, her friend helps toss them away.
Rabbit prays and prays. The pines shush his fears.

Rabbit Food sweats. They are in Claremore. Her
Grandpa's appointment at the Indian Hospital was over and
they were now erasing the memory of it by rummaging in a
second hand store. Dad was tapping at the keys of a gigantic
typewriter that had been painted white. Paint clogged the key
mechanism, but Dad's face spoke volumes. How that thing
was getting back to San Francisco was anyone's guess. Mom
would be thrilled. Rabbit Food rubs the red dot on the first
knuckle of her right hand. It's an unconscious gesture. She
pokes through a pile of books: a rock hound's guide, a math
book, a handwritten journal in English and presumably
Cherokee and a three-in-one with stories of dragons. She kept
one book with her and made her way through the store:
strange furniture, ugly floor lamps and piles of clothes. She
wanted to find a tatting shuttle, a sewing box, a book of
patterns. No such thing. The smell of heat and wet cadmium
soaked into everything. Rabbit Food rubbed her finger again.

Rabbit curls into the flour drawer of an old kitchen
table. He could smell pie crust, bread dough and biscuits.
Rabbit dreams of chicken dumpling dinners: pepper and salt
and things made of dough. This is a happy table, a table with

good memories. Rabbit rolls on his back, all four paws in the air. Not an antique yet, but a valuable thing. The turned legs showed no sign of paint or varnish, the leather of the drawer pull was cracked and stiff. Still, this was a thing of beauty, this useful tool.

Rabbit Food and the Stars Aligning

Rabbit Food sips smoky tea through a spoonful of raspberry jam. It's that pedestal table in the breakfast nook that draws these behaviors up. She communes with the shadows of those past. She runs her fingers over the matching tobacco scars: one from Gran's cigarette, one from Gramp's cigar. She listens to them, remembers them, loves across time. She plays solitaire and drinks smoke and berries. The cards aren't the same cards, but they are the same brand, red-backed with deco patterning. The rose geraniums are soaking in a bowl on the stove, becoming an infusion for jelly, a delivery system for even more sugar. Sometimes she wonders how her grandparents hadn't shaken themselves to pieces with all of the fuel they consumed – and she, trained to the same, continues the tradition. Idle hands...but they never were, were they? One more game of solitaire, one more batch of jelly, one more load of laundry: she keeps busy. There are two ways to look at winning your morning game of solitaire. Either you can feel lucky for the day that you won, or you can feel that you've used up your daily luck and decide to go back to bed.

Rabbit loves smoky tea, loves raspberry jam and loves how Rabbit Food visits images through flavors. He rolls around under the table, from time to time banging a clawed foot against the pedestal, ringing the metal. He stares at Rabbit Food's legs. Feels her shifting cards in a regular way

*on the table top. Even when she's waiting or relaxing he can
feel her being busy. He smiles and taps his claws on the single
table leg: ding, ding, ding.*

Rabbit Food and her Dad are driving around north-
eastern Oklahoma. Even in a regular, structured city Dad
could find the most bizarre, most circuitous path available.
In the country there was rarely any telling where they were.
Worse, he hadn't spent tons of time in the area for about 30
years so some of the roads he knew weren't roads anymore.
This one was doing alright, but Rabbit Food had no blessing
clue where they were. They could be headed for the Devil's
Promenade or Eureka Springs... well, not Eureka Springs. If
they were nosing into Arkansas there would be taller trees.
She was hoping for a coney, maybe some suzie-qs. Dad was
telling her about the stuffed body of John Wilkes Booth and
it's tour of Oklahoma via a 10 in 1 show. Some aunt or other
had rented the owner a room at one point. Possibly it was the
same room that Bonnie and Clyde had hired not long before
their dramatic deaths. Her aunt's rented rooms were one of
those zones of confluence; important things, people and
objects were drawn there. Nothing fey about her corner of the
family, but they were related to some strangely gifted folk. She
fiddled with the fringe on her purse, tied a knot. As they
headed along the road she realized where they were: just near
Step's Ford. On their left there was an odd sight. The field was
edge to edge with small, colorfully striped, outhouse-sized
structures. She looked at Dad, raised an eyebrow — the very
image of late teen sarcasm. Dad shrugged. The legendary
beach dressing room graveyard, perhaps. Something in the
world has a sense of humor.

*Rabbit was giggling on the floor of the rental car. Even
the rhythmic bumping over potholes was worth this moment.*

He didn't know what the little huts were, but the sight of them was hilarious, cheerful, quirky. It went with the ongoing story that Rabbit Food's Dad was unfolding. True or not, the fact that people paid to see that body: that was magic that one of his family must have arranged. It was horrible, and history is that close in Oklahoma. Rabbit Food is an example her own self. Cousin, Granddaughter, descendent of humorists, train robbers, madams, judges and what-all. There are responsibilities that have to be mediated by momentarily silly sights. He's brought them here to see the field. Little stripy houses in long, long grass, love and whimsy in equal measure. All things can be found in country fields if you know where to look. He stares at the sky out the window, watches some cousin of thunder stir clouds like river water. He sucks air and tastes Oklahoma, good red earth, the sleeping goddess that keeps tornados away, tastes the continued existence that a sense of humor had bought his folk. He rediscovers an adoration of Rabbit Food in that moment and buries his face in the sweater she's tossed onto the seat. Tears star his eyelashes. Even Rabbit gets tired sometimes. The clouds swirl and predict, swirl and predict.

Rabbit Food holds a pinch of dried tobacco between her fingertips. She offers it to this river. Long Person slides through history, travels next to human persons, and is prone to mischief. She sings to this east-running river. The tobacco is precious, grown from seeds out of an archeological site in upper Minnesota, mnis hota, a name that speaks to rivers. The tobacco had been a gift, a tiny cloth bag of it, partly in exchange for a difficult bit of beadwork. Things find a way to come back, if time is important to them, if people are listening. Long Person slides past the museum, under Tower Bridge, past the old pub behind her. She is a guest, she has a gift, a song. Rabbit Food sings. She sprinkles dried tobacco, proves to the river that she can time travel too. She turns to walk with Chestnut Man along the scrap of sand. There are bits of corroded glass, scraps of slate in various colors. There is a shell. There is trash. Like much of London this bit of beach is all about showing how little it cares about outsider opinion. The river accepts her gift, flecks of dried tobacco floating out to meet the wash from a fast boat or sink into the sucking water. None of the flecks land back on the beach. Rabbit Food thanks the river and insists on a public kiss from her man. 'Older and wiser', she thinks, 'take the kisses when you want them, when you can.'

Robin/Fox/Rabbit was hanged here once, on this very beach. It had been a finer morning than this one. Now it was spitting a little. The chill creeps up from the river and pools around their feet. Robin shivers. The day he was hanged had been clear and hot. The smell of the river in the heat was foul, bracing. He could still smell it, the varied and undisguised effluvia of a growing London. He could feel the rope around his neck, could hear the blessing spoken, felt himself fall. He couldn't remember if he'd deserved it that time. Robin/Fox/Rabbit laugh out loud. The cold creeps up.

Tides

Rabbit Food doesn't remember when they took the water fountain out of the lower yard of the school. For fifteen minutes every few hours she waits politely in a long line with the others by the gym bars. They wait for the opportunity to flip over the bar once, then take their place back in the line. When the bell rings they run to the water fountain for a last sip   before returning to the schoolroom. She pulls her long, chestnut and honey hair back with one hand while operating the fountain handle with the other. The reward is water so cold it hurts her overlarge elementary school teeth. Maybe in second grade, maybe in third grade the school took the decision to remove the fountain and to put the bars up too high for use. Neither choice was explained. It certainly couldn't be safety. The only remaining part of the fountain is a pipe that sticks about three feet out of the concrete, the cut end sharp enough to draw blood. It is always full of water. Rabbit Food taps and pounds on the pipe day after day, watching the ripple patterns, the splash patterns. Roses of water blooming in the jagged pipe end.

Rabbit sings a song of flowers, of fluid dynamics to cold water in the remains of a pipe. Rabbit eats flowers. He tucks flowers behind his ears. He makes strings of daisies from tiny flowers growing in grassy areas – sliding stems into slits in other stems. He drapes chains of flowers around himself, makes himself fabulous with flowers. Decorations, snacks:

flowers are a major part of the stuff of being Rabbit. Rabbit
dances and sings a rabbit flower song.

Rabbit Food frowns at the way the shampoo suds up.
'Hard water,' Chestnut Man had said, 'mineral salts.' These
salts collect in the electric kettle in what Chestnut Man calls
'fur'. She stirs the bathwater with one finger in a clockwise
direction, the direction of dancing, the direction of weaving
and the direction of her tatting: knot after knot. Looking into
the eye of the water, Rabbit Food sings an old song of water.
The water in the song is different. The water in London isn't
the water in San Francisco or the water in Tar Creek, but in
some ways all water is the first water she knew. She scoops up
a handful of East End tap water and looks, looks deep. Then
Rabbit Food finishes her communion, finishes bathing –
that Ani Yun Wiya obsession so noted by early British visitors.
The Cherokee river cult was still remarked upon in early
Bureau of Ethnology reports: something strange those other
people do, all that bathing. Rabbit Food goes to water, stirs
the water, sings water.

Rabbit stares into the electric kettle, scoffs. 'Fur indeed'.
His gaze is joined by that of Fox and Robin.

'It's just water,' says Fox as Robin nods.

'No such thing,' says Rabbit.

Rabbit Food is, at most, ten. She crawls out on the
deadfall. Below on the mirror of this calm stretch of creek
striders make magic with surface tension. She thinks of
letting herself fall, thinks about staying on the log. The limbs
of the deadfall are oak poem, but she doesn't read oak. She
doesn't think she's decided either way, on or off, but the shock
of water at speed knocks the air out of her when she falls, the
rest of the trip is a soft slide under the surface, like sliding

under her crocheted afghan. Rabbit Food lies on the bed
there. Watching the dimples of the striders above her, their
shadows write water-walking songs across her skin. She isn't
scared, she isn't breathing. She doesn't want the air until she
is dragged into it. Her green double knit polyester bell
bottoms stream, leaving a trail. Her cuffs gather dust as they
walk her back to the car. Rabbit Food closes her eyes and
thinks about looking up into the air, about walking on the
water.

*Rabbit smiles. This one is always running an
experiment: fluid dynamics, velocity from a deadfall, the
attraction that dry things suffer for moisture. Green and
white houndstooth pants full of creek will attract dust and
create mud. Good building material, mud.*

Near the dam spillway there is a fantastic swimming
hole. The dam makes choking noises, gurgling noises. There
are carp the size of Rabbit Food down there somewhere. Here
in the sun, near the surface, the water is blood-warm. Her
brother stirs brushpiles. Disturbs snakes. Rabbit Food stirs
water. In her denim shorts and yellow t-shirt she swims.
Swims into the fast part of the spillway and pitches her energy
against the current. Flower petals scatter as each hot burst of
wind rustles the tree branches, the trees sing about heat,
about growing near warm water. After swimming, clothes
still heavy, they buy pop at the store that also sells bait. The
temperature shift from outside to inside is nearly 20 degrees,
enough to make Rabbit Food dizzy. The pop is reservation
tepid, even though they are not on the reservation as far as
she knows. She shivers as they count coins onto black
linoleum. She shivers until they reenter the outdoors, the
heat, the smell of blooming trees.

Rabbit licks the pulltabs from their pop. He is careful, but he likes the taste of the strawberry soda. The smells of wet children, wet shoes, wet shorts and car floor surround him and he sings. He makes a new song about strawberry pop after swimming. The hiss and slight bubble as the tab ring is angled up, the crackle as the metal tongue is released, the ongoing creek water burble of carbonation against can, the taste of an idea of strawberry on a rabbit tongue. New stories are so specific: the edges of just-carved stone or the split of a just-torn nail. Rabbit seeks that pink flavor on the pulltab.

The pool is empty but for Rabbit Food. She cuts back and forth across the deep end. She enjoys the way her shoulders roll. She doesn't breathe until the other side of the pool and the flip turn. Back and forth until her teacher comes. She is tested. Treads water, arms moving, stirring chlorinated pool, stirring rarified San Francisco water — fancy pool at the medical school water. Hers only because her mother paid for the teacher. Her arms and legs move. The pool drains make slurping, gulping noises as she is timed. She watches the water swirl away from her fingers, like koi in the tea garden, like ink in Pacific. She can do this forever, until the water takes her to pieces. She passes the test.

Rabbit hates chlorine. He spends the hour in the bookstore upstairs. Because he is annoyed he swaps the contents of pencil lead ampoules. He sets copies of Star Wars upside down in the C-3PO display. Eventually he calms and stares out the window of the café. He can see the playground, the whole of the park and the Golden Gate. Fog clings like fur to the tips of the towers, to the margins of Marin. Rabbit breathes deep.

Translations

Rabbit Food restrings her aunt's coral beads. This is the aunt who seduced the married man, had a daughter who ran away. Rabbit Food, as is often the case, ties knots. A woman with many names, this aunt tells winter stories, breathes winter and eats all of the pasta. Rabbit Food imagines a straw-dolly sinking under black water, ties hope for warmth into the strand. She licks her fingers before each knot, half-listens to tales of thunder, of ram-horned serpents, stories from a home her aunt has never visited. Coral beads cross each other, lock into place with knots: coral beads from Great Great Aunt Anna. Cultural gifts convey responsibility, but this aunt doesn't know that. She tries to be patient, this woman's name doesn't translate into English and it's the only language the woman speaks. Potential ice crackles in the air of the kitchen.

Rabbit had been hoping for Easter bread. Plenty of vinegar herring, but Rabbit Food has been busy doing other things, hasn't baked. Rabbit sulks. He sits under the bay laurel tree, stares at the abandoned hummingbird nest, sturdier than he suspected for a thing of spider web and lichen. The web was gathered from around Rabbit Food's window, made by one of those thumb-sized orange and brown spiders that just showed up a few years back. The spider only marginally smaller than the hummingbird. Rabbit frets. The new nest is going into the stand of bamboo

by the other fence. He can see the male doing aerial tricks, an
emerald, ruby and taupe smear against the sky.

Rabbit Food is a child of the Bone Moon, month of
honoring family members who have passed. To say it another
way: Rabbit Food was born in February, often one of the
bitterest months for weather. In San Francisco it is usually
sunny and mild on her birthday. There is cake, there are
candles. Birds nest. Rabbit Food goes to dinner with her
family. She eats clam pizza. She eats veggie curry. She eats
Udon. She brings leftovers home that are never quite as
extensive as she remembers. A certain rabbit munches
happily. In February, from the top of Rabbit Food's hill, the
color of the bay is clearly visible, easy to see if it's green — tide
going out, or blue — tide coming in. The sun is at an angle
that paints the buildings pink at dawn, that never touches
the north side of Gran's house. Every so often the wild, single
white rose in her Gran's garden blooms on her birthday. One
year she finds a flat river stone, a skipping stone, with a mark
like a rabbit print on it.

Rabbit sings to the wild rose bush for weeks. He has the
perfect gift for Rabbit Food this year. He dances to himself,
sings to the trees and plants. He sings early spring, early
spring and joy and dancing. Raises water in the stems. There,
under the primroses, under the blue daisy things whose
name he never remembers, underneath where it stays cool
and moist, bloodroot breaks ground. Rabbit is euphoric. He
has done it, this plant doesn't grow here. He stops, still for a
moment. 'Good song, I'll have to remember that one,' then
goes on coaxing, loving, emoting. Rabbit gives away
everything. This time he hasn't fallen on his heart. This time
he's just happy, happy, happy.

The tea table is hideous. Carved wood, mostly in scrolls and fat cherubs, stained a dark brown and topped with a glass tray. To make it even more horrible, the thing is scarred with deep, lighter colored scratches from some family conflict. Rabbit Food has somehow edited this story, she has no memory of how the thing got scratched, no memory of its place in the family narrative. It's simply a battered, overblown, tacky eyesore. It crouches in her bedroom, one of those gifts you can't sell or fix or give away. She looks up from knot tying and sees it. She shudders. She wonders sometimes if it would be possible to hand the blasted thing over to some family member or other who would appreciate the gesture. Her favorite cousin has too refined a sense of taste. She ponders. It's not as if Rabbit Food doesn't enjoy family heirlooms. She still uses the wooden rolling pin with green handles. Five generations of women in her family have used that pin. It's conditionally hers now. Maybe it's about use, about tools, maybe those are the objects she honors, the stories she   remembers. The tea table perches near her couch, its horrible curled legs braced against her antipathy.

Rabbit tastes the table and spits, it tastes like evil. He turns his gaze to books, books can be fun to chew. He pulls a favorite from the shelf, The Bed Book by Dr. Seuss. Every night he used to hear this read. She loved it when she was small: the birds with their tape and bricks, the seed salesmen. She reads it these days from time to time when she's afraid that her whimsy is fading. 'Not on my watch,' thinks Rabbit. He sighs as he brushes against the horrible table again, wonders if he can arrange an accident for it. This thing would impact anyone's whimsy.

Microwaves are a miracle. Rabbit Food heats the butter to room temperature before creaming it and the sugar; just room temperature and no more. She smiles as she works, hums an old charm song she's adjusted to cover cookie baking. She misses Chestnut Man, but it has to be like this for now. She adds violet extract to the proto-shortbread. The scent of it plays hide-and-seek with her sense of smell. She remembers something about Josephine and Napoleon. A fleeting, unformed thought. They'd named some ancestor after Napoleon, called him Pole: Pole Rowe. Laughing she thinks, 'And people think I talk in strings of free association. They should hear the things I edit.' Rabbit Food adds flour, works it into the sugar and butter with a fork. She thinks about how many places in London are named to commemorate Napoleon's downfall: Nelson's column, Waterloo Station, Waterloo Gardens, pubs, hotels and monuments. She might fail to mention the relative named for him when next she is there. She works the dough into a large patty on the cookie sheet and marks where she will cut the cookies apart. As they bake the smell of violets gets stronger. She sings her cookie charm. Chestnut Man might not get to eat any of these cookies, but they are being made for him.

Rabbit is reminded of violets. Goes out to the garden, under the stairs. The white violets her Grandma had planted have gone rogue. They cover a square yard of ground. The violet flowers hide under the leaves, and there are many of them. Rabbit prefers roses, but he likes violets too. He munches happily, contemplating cookies to come. He rolls the flavor around in his mouth, it's stronger on an intaken breath. Rabbit snuggles into the patch of violets and looks up at grey clouds. Warm, fed, happy. Spring is good.

Conjurings

Rabbit Food and her brother are wearing every bit of their cold weather clothing. They have further been packaged – rigid as overstuffed teddy bears padded, as they are by unfamiliar, and usually unneeded sweaters, coats and boots – into the odd green station wagon. They head for Stow Lake in the park. Here in California on a temperate peninsula, here where it snows at most every seven years like some strange atmospheric version of an insect plague, here the man-made lake in the park is iced-over. Clearly something to see. Over 17th, down Stanyon, along Lincoln: they drive the most direct route to the lake, pull up by Rabbit Food's favorite stone bridge.

Rabbit is from a warm place. Not that it never gets chilly, just that usually it's pretty comfortable. Rabbit loves comfort, courts it. What is broken in the human mind that they need to run towards whatever passes for an extreme for wherever they live? It's warm in the house, it's cold in the park; let's all go to the park. He rolls his eyes. Rabbit Food looks like she's wearing a gingerbread girl costume: arms and legs rigid. Her hood is edged in long white wispy faux fur. 'Something has been hunting muppets,' thinks Rabbit. He hopes that they take pictures that can be used later for comedic purposes. Monkeys are hilarious.

Iced-over is a bit of an exaggeration. There is fairly solid ice around the edges of the lake; the piece Rabbit Food picks up is nearly an inch thick. Towards the middle of the lake it doesn't seem frozen at all. This is more than a rimed cat bowl, but less than a skating rink. Cold is cold... this is only seriously chilly. Her knit gloves get soaked. The faked up waterfall is switched on, possibly to avoid frozen pipes, and the water seems to fall in slow motion. Rabbit Food listens. Even though this water isn't frozen, each splash is shattered glass. She is nearly, nearly hearing something else. She wants to sit here for a while by this filthy man-made lake and listen to the water, but there is an agenda. They are bundled back into the car and whisked off to Gran's to talk about the weather. Aside from the dirt the chunks are not measurably different from what comes out of the freezer, so Rabbit Food keeps quiet and listens from in front of a heater vent as everyone marvels. She closes her eyes and pretends she's still listening to the water. She can almost feel the red and white beads between her fingers.

Rabbit sings an old song, but it doesn't mean that he isn't ready for new songs. Dawn moves across the horizon, angles differently. A city song begins in his claws, in his cocoa- and cookie-full belly. City song made of half-hearted ice on a man-made lake, ice in the freezer, cold ice-melt water soaking a little girl's gloves and a heater vent to warm up with after. He sings to the water, hears the hydrogen and oxygen spinning: Rabbit sings the B-flat of chaos, the B-flat of cities. Rabbit calls an overtone in the heater nook.

Rabbit Food and her brother put ice into their Jolly Olly Orange drink. She has hers in the plastic strawberry cup with the paint rubbed off. They use up all of the ice, start making it in sheets: fake ice instead of fake lake. They eat the sheet ice while watching the Banana Splits. For one birthday, Rabbit Food is given a kit to make the Split's dune buggy. Bingo never quite fits together properly. She gets bored and goes outside to sharpen Popsicle sticks on the sidewalk or to sit in her favorite reading tree, or to hide in the dog house. She reads, she ties knots, she drinks Funny Face drink from plastic cups shaped like anthropomorphized fruit. Strawberries — designed by the Thunder boys — a mug with a goofy face.

Rabbit watches strawberries reinvented. Sometimes he wonders what she is thinking, this girl. How does she juggle so many stories at once. It's a song in B-flat again — echoing back from corners and starting the dance. Words spin in at least three languages. Rabbit's eyes half close. One banana, two trays of ice, three Popsicle sticks sharpened to points and four hours of afternoon kid's TV. He chews a fizzy, instant soda tablet from the five-and-dime. Samples a Sweet Tart Heart, licking it cuts his tongue. New chemistry, new stories: it is the age of plastic and mail-in offers. Rabbit watches the New Arabian Nights and contemplates the human condition.

Off Fleet Street, in a little courtyard surrounded by law-related establishments, stands the Temple Church. It's raining, not enthusiastically but persistently. The door from Fleet Street is painted black. The paint is thick and the door is imposing. This isn't the East End, nor even Essex. This church doesn't care if you find it or not. There is a doorman standing by as you pass through. There is a walk down a bit of an incline. The church is round, some of the churchyard remains. Repairs from the blitz show like stretch marks on its rounded form. It crouches here, stone and carvings. Rabbit Food thinks about the Templars, about Friday the 13th, which today is not. She listens to the breathing of a building that knows who it is. Anachronism reabsorbed, rethought. Symbolic paraphernalia from the original Crusades cradled in the bosom of London. Adjustments burned away by Hitler's bombs, the punishment cell is visible now, only a few steps down inside the church.

   Rabbit/Fox/Robin, their views on organized religion well known, follow at a distance. Robin particularly finds this bit difficult, the stories of his Crusade adventures were added to the canon late, but he feels every one. 'Ah Jaques, what did they do?' He strokes the walls, bows his head at the stone images arrayed on the floor. His eyes prickle. Post-war this building is even harder for him. Closer to the original than it was for centuries, it reminds him of one of his transitional moments. He watches Rabbit Food, for once not thinking about cookies or theft. Robin starts to sing.

Adventures

It doesn't matter where they are going. It's early and they are on the California freeway in that bizarre green station wagon or maybe in the MG. It is a time when cars exist in many colors, and here in California they do indeed, confetti-bright scraps screaming along the road. It is before the seat belt laws and she bounces around in the back. Scanning for other cars, competing in this relaxed race... this slow dance in the Morning Red. Heading south on 101, she is manic in the way that children are manic when Daddy pulls them from bed at an odd hour. She is a remora; along for the ride, along for the scraps. Play her cards right and she may get forbidden food. Once it was Mountain Dew and orange Zingers; nauseating as a breakfast, but delightfully contraband. It is Dad, smoking in the front seat. It is out of the house at dawn when she would otherwise be hearing the bus as a dinosaur and quaking under her hand crocheted lavender afghan and yellow blankets. It is adventure.

Rabbit doesn't approve of things that disturb his sleep unless they are his idea. Who takes a child out at this hour? South and through some of the creepiest stories in the west. West, the direction we go in death; and didn't the Spanish reinforce that? Didn't the U.S.? Don't they still? Rabbit shudders, feeling old as he usually does not. Even jesters have a hard time making sense of some of these histories and the mission bells march in lines down the freeway. He looks out the window and sees men, their legs painted in stripes. He can hear clackers. He thanks them for their hosting, thinks thoughts of love and strength to them. He is a Southeastern guest and will mind his manners. He listens to the songs and dances as they get nearer. The songs come back, they come back, clack, clack, clack.

The kids are asleep and so is the man next to her. Rabbit Food tries to breathe in a way that won't wake him. She tries to hold her body still. She pretends to sleep, hoping that the pretence will become reality. When she feels him start to stir she gives up and goes downstairs for tea. Both the cat and the parrot are offended by her intrusion into the night time house. The stove light dazes her. She begins to assemble ingredients, not knowing what she's preparing for until she takes an egg out of the refrigerator. Cookies at 3am. She blames an audacious bunny for the impulse — begins to cream butter and sugar.

Rabbit steals an almond from the already annoyed parrot and nibbles as he watches her fumble her tea together. He didn't teach her insomnia, though he approves of the way she uses the time. He watches her finely chop a handful of just-picked rosemary, separate an egg, wrap the dough in clingfilm. He steals half an avocado from the fridge and thinks tortilla thoughts at her.

Night sounds and the air is swamp. She can't sit in the living room: the cousins and uncles are all in sleeping bags there. She puts the lamp on the lowest setting and looks for a book. There is a bible, lives of the saints and a collection of children's stories in 20 volumes of various graying colors. She would go drive, go to the river, if she could leave the house, but there are too many sleeping between her and the door.

Grateful for the room to herself, packed as it is with things that have no place of their own, she flips through the first book of the series. Adventure stories pour out, travel: boats and trains and rafts and wagons and horses. In a family with stories like ours, buying adventure books... She thinks about Rufus, first getaway car driver in Oklahoma. Sadly it was in a time when a fit man could outrun a car but, an innovator nevertheless – my family. She thinks of her Grandfather chasing Rommel around North Africa. She thinks of him in this last year. She slides the window open and barely avoids cricket spit through the screen.

Rabbit rolls under the open hide-a-bed. He finds an old gumdrop stuck to the rug and chews at it. He can hear the Thinkers coming in from Denver. They will be at this funeral too. He watches his girl as she remembers the songs of this part of the world. Her hair curls into smiles in the humidity. Her Grandfather's death was a blessing at this point, impossible to sing that song yet, but she knows it too. He sings softly to remind her of the place: love, safety, community... cricket spit. The air crackles, she will tie knots again soon, he can taste it. She smells of spicebush, of wet air, of the thread.

Jet-lag, the rain wakes her. In his sleep Chestnut Man pulls her to him, just tight. He breathes sleep into her hair, against her neck. It's a spell that isn't working. She tries, arranging herself against his long body. She is small here in his arms, small and warm. He becomes her book, her heater vent, a white formica table in a room with mustard and green wallpaper. Even so – her cells, her chemicals, scream at her to move, to rove the night house, perhaps to bake. She extracts herself, heads for the kitchen and tea. She wonders how the floor in that one room can be so perishing cold. Fortunately the electric kettle is quick. She takes her tea to the living room. She sits on the couch they fixed together, flicks through channels. She picks up a story-thread: vintage British TV drama. Rabbit Food begins again to collect words, knot them into stories, she takes up the thread.

Rabbit/Fox/Robin are indignant that there are no cookies being baked. Bodie and Doyle aside, if you aren't baking or sneaking there is no reason to be awake in the night. A drunken lover's spat outside distracts them, then a soft fall of rain. The lady has taste in nights anyhow. Rabbit sings to the rain, sings softness the sidewalk, to the lovers who are now quiet. Rabbit catches her thread and spins, and spins.

Transformations

Caresses

Chestnut man drives Rabbit Food to the airport. They wind through Islington, past trees just breaking bud. It seems ungrateful to be going back to San Francisco when Chestnut Man had just finished making spring. Rabbit Food sighs. She knows this drive too well, the curve around London. They pass St. Pancras, Victorian confection that always reminds her of Moorish architecture. She presses her hand on his thigh. Not ready to go, not ready to go. She feels like a small child, mutinous, resistant. She has to be somewhere in San Francisco in a few days. They pass the bust of Jack Kennedy, she keeps meaning to look up that story... still doesn't know why that thing is there. Rabbit Food is greedy, greedy for these moments with Chestnut Man, greedy for these unfamiliar narratives. She wants to know all of the little spirits of this old old place, how to be a good guest to them. She wants to be in London for warm weather some day. Warm weather in London is a myth that Chestnut man shares with her: days without an extra sweater, maybe even days when her hair wouldn't frizz from the drizzle. There are museums, corners, parks to explore. She isn't done. She wants to wake up with her man, the silence of his house to work in, the press of his wild creativity against her own. She wants to scream, so she sings very quietly, she sings a small song of patience and tries to convince herself.

Robin and Fox are agreed. This woman of Rabbit's is polite. Rabbit shrugs; he'd always seen her as a bit sharp, but supposes that this isn't what they mean. A honeybee settles on one of his ears and he starts in suspicion. She sits still and so does Rabbit. Things have started to come out to see him, drawn by his Rabbit charm. There are quiet things here, things built over. It's a good place for his thread spinner, she likes it here. It's beginning to like her. Small beings watch her leave this time, have become alert to her peregrinations. They take hold of her imagination as Rabbit watches, they tug at her. He's thinking of her, but of himself too. Easy to fall for this place. He wonders if Rabbit Food has packed fruit sherbets for him, or maybe black currant licorice. Rabbit doesn't want to go home either. He sings a low harmonic.

Rabbit Food drives the shovel into just-turned dirt and looks over her work. Nearly half of the garden weeded and turned. The plum tree and the rose bushes look dubious, but it's going to be amazing. A dozen frais du bois sit in temporary pots next to ten lavender plants. Each lavender is different. They are pink, blue, an array of purples, even green and white. There are also ten creeping thyme plants. She arranges the various plants where she thinks that she wants them. Strawberries, lavender and thyme: she smiles. This is happy labor. Plant after plant is coaxed out of its pot, gets a light root massage and is nestled into the soil. Rabbit Food turns the hose gently on each. She is picturing sleep pillows, mushroom and barley soup and strawberries taken one at a time and eaten right there.

Rabbit assumes a louche posture among the saffron crocuses. The smell reminds him of last year's rice dinner and he smiles. He stares up at a plum tree full of fingertip, green, set plums. Soon they will be yellow, the size of ping-

pong balls. Soon they will be sweet. He angles his head back and watches Rabbit Food. She digs well for a human person, and to good effect. He gazes longingly at the wild strawberry plants. He remembers the Thunders creating them: the husband's need to lure back his angry wife. Forgiveness is good, but not as good as just-picked strawberries. Lavender meant not just the pillows that Rabbit Food was imagining now, but also flower flavored shortbread. Rabbit wriggles. Thyme would flavor sorbet and salad dressing. It would be fun to roll in on sunny days. Rabbit chews at plum bark in excitement. He really must learn songs to charm lavender and thyme. He already knows how to charm strawberries, that is a song he's been singing for years.

Rabbit Food is reading about the Mary Celeste. She loves that there are unknown things. She reads crypto-zoology texts as well, believes that gators and crocs are getting bigger, believes in giant squids. She sighs; later in the book they discuss Roanoke. No mention is made of her blue-eyed Lumbee cousins on the mainland. Mystery indeed. She puts down her book and takes up some partial lace. Rabbit Food ties knots of solving un-mysteries, of making simple the difficult. She ties knots of renaming, knots against resistance to complicated explanations for the Ohio River Valley mounds. Between these she ties knots of embracing the unknown, of endless and vivid possibility. Rabbit Food dances these knots in a clockwise direction. Rabbit Food dreams.

Rabbit watches spider weaving and begins to sing stories. He sings about musicians learning about warmth of a note, about coolness of a note. Rabbit sings about throwing small wooden boats across oceans, about the dance of DNA. Songs about tall storytellers tattooed with marvelous animals mix with songs of years-old seeds sprouted. Rabbit sings of tinfoil hats and violet perfume. Rabbit sings songs of things likely and unlikely. Every story is true. He can tell that Spider is listening. He loves her perfect gestures, her accurate measuring. He loves her webs so much that he wants to dance through them, to be caught by her. She keeps one eye supervising him as she has since the first dawn: serious as always, suspicious as always. Rabbit moans, hugs himself thinking of the joys of being woven into her web. He moans that she has never loved him back. Rabbit's fantasies unrequited, he wanders off to see what his girl is doing. As he leaves Spider sings one of his songs softly and smiles to herself. Spider adjusts a thread and sings a song of floppy ears and disorder and a crooked mammal smile.

Evasions

The rain comes and Rabbit Food becomes a quiet place, separate from the garden and later the street. The rain is a fence making her into a reservation, land set aside, the water a line drawn invisibly between her and other things, other people. She picks her way to the school, the larger arena where people are all thrown in together. Today's origami lesson is a toy, the teacher's favorite, but there are a few tricky points. This class is amazing, attentive, a few of them have an intuitive understanding of the geometry. Rabbit Food explains as though she were giving out cookies, each bit of information a treat. Maybe this group will learn to love math as many do not, as she does herself. They make the toy and play.

Rabbit chews on the edges of paper. Rabbit Food's classes are one of his not most favorite things about her. He didn't bother to work out why. Teaching twenty kids at a time how to make toys out of an easily accessible material was a caper that should appeal to him. Maybe it was the kids, city kids tend to have more structured lives, even the ones whose lives you wouldn't trade for bottle caps. He liked the breakfast that the teacher brought for her though. He usually got pastry, which she never bought for herself anymore. Rabbit gnaws book edges selectively, trying to reuse already printed letters to create new words. She always did like school more than he did.

Cold and bright, the day jars Rabbit Food. She has a pile
of things to do and doesn't want to do any of them. She
stretches on her bed. It's hard to give ones self a day off when
self-employed, but today is one of those days. She decides to
go for a walk to and in Golden Gate Park. Pink shirt, black
sweater and wool coat; she pulls on a pair of fingerless mitts.
It gets truly cold in this city only often enough for people to be
cranky about it. It's not like London, where the cold becomes
a badge of endurance, a main topic of conversation. Here
people just put one more layer on and wander around looking
confused and betrayed. The light on the buildings is painfully
bright. Its bounce off of the ocean is worse as she crests the
hill near 17th. Rabbit Food winces. The recent rains have
mulched the eucalyptus leaves and made the sidewalk
dangerously slippery. She picks her way carefully down the
other side of 17th to Cole Street. Women come and go from
the yoga parlor, each shivering, looking indignant and
surprised at the chill. Across the street apples — black, pink,
green — nestle in fancy baskets. Perfect berries of all kinds
seduce from thick green cartons. The exotic fruit indicates the
general income level of the neighborhood, a far cry from the
1960's. Even the antique houses have changed, many of them
painted some variation of beige these days, rather than the
peacock colors of her childhood. She moves past them
towards the scent garden in the park.

Rabbit licks his lips at the sight of the fruit. He has
always craved perfection; exotic or no. He knew that there
would be plants he would eat in the Arboretum. He trails
after Rabbit Food, north and west. He window shops. He
people watches. Skinny women and gym-toned men file past
them. They are well groomed, clear skinned, carefully dressed
— if sometimes carefully disheveled. Crossing streets

punctuates their walk, expensive fruit and bath oil give way to used clothing and exotic restaurants. Coffee shops offer jewel-like pastry. Stationary, tortured silver and semi-precious stones, elixirs and potions that reportedly stave off aging: Rabbit Food barely notices any of it, but Rabbit sees everything. They march towards stands of eucalyptus, of trees, bushes and incidental plants either put there by the citizens of San Francisco or descended from plants that had been. There was a Rabbit sensibility to the tumble of vegetation in this park. As they enter it, he smiles. Rabbit thinks of rolling in pepper scented pelargoniums.

Rabbit Food is small. Her father has hoisted her to his shoulders. This is a mixed experience, she doesn't like being up so high and digs her hands into his hair, sticky baby fists clenching in monkey reflex. The air in the hothouse is as advertised: hot and wet. He walks her across the bridge over the lily pond. This image of controlled water indoors would find its way into her dreams for years to come. White, waxy blossoms float with light purple and pink cousins on the surface of the murky liquid. Above her, whitewashed glass filters light. Her father lurches under her again, she feels panic and euphoria. Lit by this breath of overcharged oxygen, the exhalations of contained plants, Rabbit Food shudders. She stares at the lily pond, sees olive, white, orange and black shapes sliding under the surface. Since seeing them she will never be able to cross bridges close to water without a shiver of concern, though she forgets why. She presses her face into her father's thick black curls.

Rabbit sneaks happily in the warm wet. This glass house is more like his home country than anything else on this coast. He teases Rabbit Food's underwater monsters, koi obscured by huge lily leaves. He breathes deep. There is a difference between captive water and wild water. These cascading Victorian basins are compelling though. Plant zoo, but the plants don't seem to mind an easy life. Manicured, pampered, fed; the flora here bloom hugely, grow straight, keep schedules. Rabbit nibbles them a bit, lovingly, to remind them what life is in the outside world. Some were grown from seed, never knew the fuss, bustle and comforting struggle of life in the rainforest. Some of the inmates were brought from cloud forest, from that world of heat and wet and insect and strangler fig. Rabbit breathes deep of the maypop scent. Some things will always be missed. This tidy leaf litter, this carefully managed balance, it becomes suddenly depressing and Rabbit is glad that they are leaving these aristocratic pets to their whitewashed light.

Discoveries

Rabbit Food walks through Pall Mall, location of
gentlemen's clubs, also formerly of the War Office and the
Temple of Health and Hymen. She is surrounded by stone
and networking. Close to both the park and Regent Street.
Nothing surprises her about the club of science kink that
once occupied Schomberg House. London of stone and brick
is possessed by some minor goddess of conflicted sexuality.
Schomberg House was divided, housed a bookstore, parts of
the War Office, other things over the years — all related, it
seemed to Rabbit Food. Small shocks and large are bracing,
able to pull people out of routine a bit. Rabbit Food, in search
of beads, in search of thread to knot — threads of story —
finds knots already here in Pall Mall. Knots neatly tied off and
not needing anything from her, thank you very much. Rabbit
Food finds that she likes the tumble of market place better,
likes the small, allowable chaos of the canal locks, and if she's
honest, she likes her kink a bit less controlled as well. She
sends a mental blessing to temples of the past and heads
off to the tumble and heat of her new favorite fabric store, a
celebration of sensuality that doesn't require the validation
of a fancy address. Her fingers ache to stroke living cloth, to
be surrounded by wanton color; she sings a small song to
the phallic column of the Duke of York c. 1834. She offers a
pinch of tobacco to the unnamed deity and wanders off to
Regent Street.

Rabbit is off at platform 10, King's Cross station. He sits, eats the first white plum blossom of the season and ponders the overthrow of wicked invaders. He closes his eyes and remembers the smell of waist length red hair, of woad body paint and rage. He traces in his mind the constellations of freckles on her shoulders and cheeks, remembers them crossed with marks of the Roman whip. Her rage lit the countryside. Rabbit presses his paws against the floor. He can feel the mud under his paws as he predicted each of her victories, none of them quenching her need for release until he couldn't stand that need any longer. Fox reminds him that she isn't really here. Robin stands guard, as if he can still feel the battle too. Rabbit knows where her body really rests, but it matters what people think, and he chooses to remember her here, in the city she changed forever. He whispers her heart name to the final petal of his flower, and then the one everyone knew her by, Victory.

Rain and knots, Rabbit Food is edging a handkerchief for a niece-to-be that she has never met. She has painted the silk fabric in silver, a silly but compelling little pattern that can be folded to reveal a valentine heart. The lace keeps reminding her of small bones: snake ribs, mouse spine. She improvises, changes patterns. Stories unfold in the numbers that no one else will see, let alone be able to read. Sometimes Rabbit Food thinks that she is made by knots, rather than making them. Chestnut Man brings her tea flavored with bergamot and orange. He reminds her of the glasses she has just started wearing for work. Her eyes are fine, but no one is designed to use them for 12 straight hours of tiny knotting. She puts on her glasses, smiles at his now blurry, too far away form. She calls him back for a kiss, in the hope that it will help her tie affection into each knot. Medicine work takes more focus than she can muster some days, hard to do it on deadline. They won't know if she isn't focused, but she would know. She kisses Chestnut Man, nips at his lower lip, then lets him get on with his woodworking. She turns her attention back to the lace; this corner becomes spiky, vehement. She listens and ties more knots.

Rabbit seems caught in the light of a contemplative star this week. He wanders old palaces, old prisons. He finds an ancient holy well: capped off, ignored, forgotten. Rabbit curls up at the bottom of the well. The mud contains the remnants of women's prayers. Rabbit loves women. He loves them throughout time. He's often been accused of loving too much, and it's probably true. He listens quietly to old prayers, can almost hear the goddess they were made to, but she isn't here. Rabbit Food isn't interested in him at the moment, caught by a project she has shut him out. He sulks in knowing unfairness. He tastes apples, can hear bees. The goddess of this spring was all about fire and poetry. Here in the sealed dark, under history as monastery, palace, prison, Rabbit   begins to hum a morning song through the water. He answers a few of these left over prayers, small things, things   related to rabbits. Rabbit is singing again, but he's still sulking. He will stop when he is good and ready.

The boy is staring at Rabbit Food. He is dry, he is fed, they sit in a chair and he stares at her. Babies should not be so still, so focused. She had been led to believe that babies were all about needs and sleep. The boy stares. She taps his nose with a finger and he starts, crosses his eyes to look at the finger. He holds his eyes that way for a moment and then wrinkles his nose and looks back at her face. He hisses at her, gurgles: a kettle, a gator. This one has things to say. He will have to wait. He doesn't seem to be a someone who likes waiting. He doesn't grab her hair. She doesn't know why. Doesn't want him to, but has no idea how he knows that. A small hand wobbles to her nose. She arranges his fingers for him, guides the tip of his finger to the tip of her nose. The boy stares. As a teenager she'd had a kitten who hated sleeping. The kitten would play until he'd fall asleep sitting in the middle of the kitchen floor. The boy does a similar thing now. His finger touching her nose, mid-stare, the boy falls asleep. Even then his face is serious. She should go put him in his bed. Instead she holds him, heavier sleeping than awake, she holds him just for a bit longer.

Rabbit decides to create a burrow under the compost pile. His small paws churn. He is a digging machine. Dirt plumes behind him. He is born to dig. Rabbits dig, he is digging. He is utterly satisfied. He hits the inevitable clay. He is steadfast. The clay sticks in his foot fur. The clay gets between his claws. The clay is difficult. He stops, panting. He looks at the dent he's made in the dirt. This is not a burrow. He looks up at the bay tree. Maybe it's just regular rabbits that burrow. Rabbit rolls in the slightly churned clay, makes himself ruddy. He climbs the tree and drapes himself on a branch. Maybe a nest, thinks Rabbit.

Deprivations

Water is out in the East End. Rabbit Food cradles the last possible cup of tea between one hand and her chest. She would go somewhere, if the only places she wanted to go weren't within the no-water zone. She and Chestnut Man decide to do a crossword, an activity as much mind-meld as vocabulary test. She loves how he smiles when either one of them gets a difficult or obscure reference. One day she would write a letter to the Times about the romantic properties of the daily puzzle, for now she sips tea and lets her honey do the writing.

Rabbit plays in the construction site. Schematics are so easily rotated, suddenly not showing water pipes in their correct location... Rabbit splashes his paws in the new mud and listens to construction men. Rabbit learns words. He had not known that that particular pipe would fountain quite so spectacularly, or that it would leave a fourth of London without water. Shifts of perspective aren't bad, particularly in a place where people take their established routines so seriously. Granted, it would have been better if it were the city; so full of the earnest, the ones who won't look at you in the tube even if you are closer, skin to skin, than their husbands or wives have been in months. Even so, it's a glorious mud puddle and Rabbit coats himself.

Fox and Robin have a moan about the Olympic construction project. No parking in the East End while the

*games are on, and everything in such uproar. Olympics, who
needs them, eh? Meanwhile one tawny haired construction
worker knows enough to scan the site for pointy muzzle and
ears. He wonders at the frolicking hare in the mud, but
doesn't see fox. Well, who knows, all kinds of things happen
on a construction site.*

Rabbit Food scans shelves full of preserved biotic
material. Transparent, translucent and/or desiccated: the
samples that had survived the blitz are arranged in glass
cases on glass shelves. It is all very scientific. There is a
seemingly sensational focus on human anomaly, and a
slightly self-aware nod at some degree of grave robbing. She
scans the bones of Caroline Crachami, a child whose time as
a sideshow draw and subsequent exhaustion probably
speeded her death by tuberculosis. The museum displays her
bones, casts of one arm and a foot, a thimble and a ring.
Rabbit Food hums a mourning song for Caroline: child of
music who would never have heard this song. There is
something wistful about the collection here. Another singer
had described certain kinds of scientists to Rabbit Food as
the sort of folk who would take the drum apart to see where
the sound came from. Rabbit Food shivers. Chestnut Man
drags her to a different room. Two Cherokee faces look out at
her, unnamed, dressed in the lavishness of wealthy men of the
time. They were beautiful, these temporally distant men,
Rabbit Food smiles. She is haunted by images of fetal long
bones, delicate as lace, tagged, cataloged and shelved. She is
haunted by the 'exotic' people in the art collection whose
names are not noted. She smiles again, there is nothing that
she can do about Caroline and her father, who cried when he
found that they were cutting up his baby girl. The Cherokee

men... she knew who would know them. Perhaps their names will be added.

Rabbit gawps at the cast bronze flowers that are the base of each banister post on the way up to the museum. The flowers are so perfect, bronze against the cream marble, that they make Rabbit hungry for something else. Rabbit understands a trickster desire to make one thing stand in for another. He understands a joy in craft and artifact. He also knows the difference between yummy flowers and things that are not flowers, the difference between life and never living. Fox and Robin are somewhere else in Lincoln's Inn. Part of Rabbit wants to be somewhere else too. He wants to sniff the complicated chimney pots, and memorize their designs. He wants to read every bit of heraldry in the Chapel. Rabbit Food needs him close, so close he is. Work work work. Tracking her he is struck by the treeness of the human lung, a model made by filling the voids with something, some plastic. We are all trees at one level or another, muses Rabbit. He is more interested in the living ones and hunts up Rabbit Food.

To call this a castle is a bit of rewrite. Nodules of unfinished flint rubble the hillside where it angles down towards the outlet of the Thames. Rabbit Food takes in the hints of curtain wall, pieces of unconvincing towers. This castle was picked apart by human corbies, shiny bits of flint used to build other things. Rabbit Food checks the view once more. Clear why an opportunist like William would have favored this place. Not only close to cockle beds — images of orange shellfish flavored with vinegar — but the view. Even with the contemporary haze you can see distances. Rabbit Food begins to be able to read these eternally damp rocks. She begins to understand somewhat the motivation behind the chess game of crowns and castles and walls and walls and walls. She shakes her head in rejection. The lord of this castle-that-had-been made war the business of his life and it was hard not to think of him as a usurper. Aristocracy, some kind of wrestling pit where close cousins fight to the death if everyone was lucky. A pretty day this, light elegant on the water. Maybe they would go have some of those cockles. Maybe they would... Chestnut Man seeks a kiss of his own accord. Rabbit Food kisses him. His people are from this place or close by since forever. On this day that passes for spring here, on this chilly, pretty day she would not fight the wars of the past. She kisses Chestnut Man near the margin of the fallen bailey.

Rabbit and Fox play with empty shells near the breakwater. There on the patio East Essex has turned out for the pretty day. Children throw the shells and they chase: taupe and white fur flashing invisibly in the surf. Rabbit Food and Chestnut Man are buying lunch at the cockle shed while seemingly all of East Essex arrays itself in the chill bright of this gift of a day. Neither Fox nor Rabbit know where Robin has taken himself, no matter. There is a high tide, there are shells and soon there will be cockles. The children make up a game with the shells and a way to keep score. The children play.

Rabbit Food is in the right side of the kitchen sink, a sink full of soapy water. She slaps her hands flat on the water and watches it fountain. The porcelain is cool under her. Her small body fits neatly as her Gran washes her. She cooperates, loves being immersed, loves the bubbles. She makes sounds at her Gran. Her Gran makes sounds at her. She slaps the water.

Rabbit hums to the lavender rose, he flirts with Spider. Spider, as always, pretends to ignore him. He strengthens the apple tree named for Rabbit Food. Its blooms are almost the color of her cheeks: ice white and light pink. She is not a creature from an old story, she is the servant of a continuing story and Rabbit very much enjoys not knowing all of the end. This apple tree, as ropy as it looks at the moment, this tree right here, will survive and give small sweet apples. Rabbit sings and sings.

Reclamations

Rabbit Food goes to the Pow Wow to see people looking beautiful, to be beautiful. It's a trick of light on glass beads. The drummers smell of sweet-flag root. The dancers smell of smoked hide. Tarp covered gym floor shivers under the truth of feet dancing. Dancers are spinning the world into equilibrium; butterfly scraps of color, fringe, yarn, finger weaving. Light spins off the rainbow of a CD repurposed as an arm ornament. Rabbit Food can smell beans, smell fry bread. She shrugs a green shawl around her shoulders and stands for the dance. Her shoes settle gently on the tarp. Michelle dances up next to her, they don't speak, they dance these new dances, dressed in new clothes. They dance and are beautiful.

Rabbit rummages in the food under the fry bread booth. His feet drum in time with an intertribal, in time with the munching of perfect tomatoes. He can feel Rabbit Food's careful feet on the pulse of the world, can feel her setting things right. She loves dancing, loves the people here and still only comes around rarely. Rabbit enjoys her pleasure, enjoys tomatoes and shredded cheddar. Rabbit sighs; it's going to be a very long night.

Rabbit Food zooms through the night. Over the Davis Strait she catches her breath. Such a long way to get to Chestnut Man... She ties knots, or tries in the strange airplane light. She rummages through the offered movies.

She glares at the cup that crouches on her tray table. Offering an apology to the demi-deities of tea she makes the steward remove the foul stuff. Rabbit Food shudders. Her eyes half close as she tries to remain herself, tries to cling to the thread, the odd single element construction: the knots, the crossings. She buries her nose in Chestnut Man's shirt. After three months of washings she can barely conjure him, but the softness of it, the gesture of him giving it, the intention comforts her. She pulls her window shade open and looks down to see moonlight catching on the sharp edges of water. That world of sound, of wounded ice groaning — that world is below and out of reach. Rabbit Food is suspended. She sits on her cushion, which — in case of a water landing — can be used as a floatation device. Her oxygen mask remains packed in its cubby above her. She is not even halfway to him. She hums a very small song about going east.

Rabbit curls into a very small ball. He is snow, he is sleet, and he is stasis. He is anything that isn't contraband to get Rabbit Food in trouble. He presses himself tighter and tighter into the corner of Rabbit Food's bag. Something oddly shaped finds itself under his happy fuzzy nose. The air on this plane has him stuffed to his eyeballs, congested utterly he cannot smell the thing. His quick bunny tongue laps it, traces its shape. Mmmmmmm. He takes it into his mouth, a cashew. He loves Rabbit Food, loves her now with the completeness that only someone thoroughly self-absorbed can achieve, and only then for small moments. A cashew is pleasure made edible. He sucks on it, shaves a tiny bit off with his lower teeth. With luck he can make it last over Greenland, over Ireland ... perhaps even to Birmingham. It's so quiet this high in the air, no one but the plane people and one or two Thunder cousins. Below him he can hear the thrum and fuss

of water things, of cold things and things that supervise cold
things. He can sense these things, but as if in another room.
Rabbit settles into a good sleep, mouth rich with cashew.

Scattered ume blossoms on the tree. The other branches
are tight, expectant with things that are nearly leaves, things
that are nearly flowers. Flowers are perched on the edge of
that hydraulic trick they do every year, water pressure and
sun become exuberance. It's misting lightly, fueling the
quivering tension in the tree. Rabbit Food sits on a chair in
the mist, leans back and lets it soften her. A medium sized
spider has strung a web between the upper and lower
clothesline. Yellow Bird and his female build a new nest,
vaguely put out that she insists on lurking so closely. The wild
rose is covered with perfect miniature rosebuds, none are
open yet. Something must have brushed the rosemary bush:
its smell is as intoxicating as the chanting mist. Errands can
wait, Rabbit Food listens.

All rabbits love spring, they are known for it. Rabbit
rambles the garden. Spider hides. Rabbit munches
sourgrass, the yellow blossoms announcing its citrus taste. A
generous plant, it reproduces hysterically in spring, covering
the garden. If you set out a pot of dirt in California you will
probably find sourgrass growing there. Sourgrass is the
vegetal rabbit. Rabbit sates himself.

Rabbit Food chases a rumor of cool down the Siq into
Petra. Echoes of Dushara flicker at the edges of her
awareness: smoke without fire. Bird planted figs grow thirty
feet up on the sandstone walls, the periodic bas relief of
Dushara's empty chair. Closing her eyes she can imagine the
trickle of water down the spillways, past the carved camel. The
Siq is cool, in shadow between halves of broken hillside. The
path shifts to Roman paving and Rabbit Food counts steps,

turns the corner and is confronted by the Treasury. Petra, a city cut from the hillside, and here, this bit carved as a temple. Dushara, lord of the mountain, continues to whisper. Now, out of the Siq, the heat comes up, rises around her with the dust. The sandstone is pink yes, but also purple and black, sunset reds folded and folded like Damascus steel. Rabbit Food shivers in the suddenly overwhelming heat, shivers and walks into the city proper. Remnant temples skew or recline, but those were later. There at the center another fig speaks to the water she can neither see nor hear. Farther in there are steps to the monastery, there is a mosaic pavement up the hill, there are toppled pillars. Vast and baking plazas are not known in that urban way of stone and stone by foot's touch. The embracing sandstone is beautiful, dry and hopeful still. Rabbit Food settles in the shadow of the fig to think and listen to the shuffling and whispering of the god of the empty chair.

Rabbit plays, bounds, hides on each of a thousand stairs. He runs in and out of doorways, sits on every seat in the amphitheatre. He finds carvings that the archeologists have not. He admires the rabbit mosaic in the temple pavement. He sings in the empty cistern, casting ripples through his own body with sound. Rabbit tries to worry at the camels, but they ignore him, only the most polite camels work here. Rabbit snorts. Petra is a warren, and he knows all about warrens. Something does shift and glide just out of reach even for him, but he's too taken with this place to coax. Wind speaks in the empty water storage cubes. Water moves somewhere under the old fountain. Rabbit plays stick game with Bedu children for scraps of purple rock. Petra of waiting, of the long view, drinks sunlight. Petra seduces.

Pilgrimages

Rabbit Food, her brother and her father, land in Tulsa in the evening. There is the usual hubbub of collecting luggage, collecting rental car. Rabbit Food sits and stares at the biplane hanging from the ceiling. She stares at the bust of a cousin that stands underneath it. Rabbit Food feels her face becoming more of a map here, unlined and moist as it is, people look at her dad, her brother, her... she feels herself transforming into something that can be understood, with or without romanticism. She breathes the thick air of an Oklahoma summer, thinner here in Tulsa, but curdling even as they head out of the terminals, angle north. She starts counting the reflective bumps on the road. She gets to 117 before she stops. Dad has found a radio station, "... no shoes, no pool, no pets." Temple complexes of cloud drift in from Denver with new prayers. There will be rain, the rivers will swell. It won't cool a thing, that rain. The radio shifts to Johnny Cash singing river magic. Rabbit Food relaxes on her seat and closes her eyes.

Rabbit happily runs through the terminals. He unties shoelaces as he goes; small potatoes for a being like him... home home home. Home? Home or what passes for it. More stately things notice, smile and move on. He stops at the sight of a truly arresting beauty. Rabbit is tempted, glances at his girl. She's entertained, surrounded by family; perhaps Rabbit could take some time for himself. He starts to sing a song of transformation, a song of blessing a comb. Rabbit combs his fur. Rabbit is transformed.

Rabbit Food is undercover. She collects her books, collects her class schedule. All they'd had to promise her was a library with more books than she could ever read. She gathers the things that she needs, takes a deep breath, and goes to see the books. Gliding through the rows and rows of shelves, Rabbit Food smiles. She strokes the spines of some of them, a promise of later intimacy. Five floors... unbelievable luxury, sexy as a dancer in new regalia. She breathes the smell, feels her feet move in a prayer dance. Rabbit Food imagines what it would be to know, to have read these constellations, these tree rings. On her way out she hooks one that she just can't do without, not for one more second.

Rabbit runs quick rings around his flower. He celebrates this beginning. Tea, books and argument: these things she enjoys so deeply, all here in one place. It's a new sharp knife for her, this education. He wonders if she will become as terrifying as the image in his mind, then he remembers and smiles. He runs in even harder circles, Rabbit celebration. He leaps and leaps. Finally, things are beginning.

They kiss slowly. His tongue slips between her lips and she timidly licks at the tip. She shivers. They are barely touching, the kisses intense but controlled. She tastes the tea he's been drinking, his soft lips warm from it still. Foghorns sound in the bay, easily audible from her hill. Rabbit Food pulls back, frames his face with her small hands. She loves this man, whatever that chemical reaction is. She wants so badly to just pull him close, closer. She wants to be without responsibility. She moans, an octave higher than the foghorns. She knows she has to get up and out. She has to

rebutton her shirt. She has to find her shoes. Her heartbeat is
everywhere in her skin. She pushes him gently away and looks
at her watch. He trails his beautiful, dexterous fingers across
her breasts, smiles at her. There is work, and she has to do it.
There is work. She takes his hands in hers. She rests her head
against his chest. She looks up. He is smiling at her. She
pushes him away again and hunts her shoe. Rabbit Food
doesn't always love being a grown-up. On her way out the
door she puts her ear buds in, calls up her favorites. Guitar
as foghorn sounds in her ears. That's not going to help.

*Rabbit dances the roofline, does a back flip. This
landscape of water and tarpaper is all potential. Three
houses up he finds a plant growing in the rain gutter. He
nibbles at it lovingly. He bounds away. Ravens pose in dignity
on the pine trees. One lovely young female watches him. He
winks at her, shifts, becomes a swamp rabbit. He ears
shorten, his color dapples a bit more. Rabbit wonders what
these Ravens might be guarding under that tree, but he has
dancing to do so he moves on without asking. Foghorns cry to
him, useless for his kind of navigations. He sniffs the air,
heads up to the spring on the hill, to the stand of the local
'tower of jewels', spectacular vegetation. He avoids dogs on the
old kite-flying hill. The blackberry tangle is thick with flowers.
He pictures his fur streaked with purple berry juice, his skin
scratched as if for dancing. No berries now, just heading for
the hill. The foghorns sing to him.*

Rabbit Food walks up Grant Avenue. The smells of dim
sum and rose soap swirl around her and the flocks of
tourists. She passes the chop-carving store on the corner,
mini teapots tangle with old cardboard and beautiful
brushes in the window. Rabbit Food basks in the fabulous
chaos of narrow streets and familiar spices. She walks quickly,

90

angling around slow moving visitors. She stops at the Orange Julius and gets a slush. Sipping she moves on. Curls of moxa scent from an upper window remind her to turn down towards the fortune cookie bakery. Thinking twice she picks up a bag of still-warm cookies for her gran. Moving still she stops at the renamed restaurant, site of a horrible multiple shooting and home of the best chicken bau in the city. She places an order: turnip cake, lop chong bau, chicken bau, pork bau and custard bau (that last not on the menu: there are things you just need to know without being told) har gau and pork siu mai finish off the list. Rabbit Food collects her pink box tied with green plastic. She looks at her watch. Twenty minutes to get to the wharf before the blues player finishes his set. She'd make it in time to hear him some. More importantly she'd make it in time to feed him. Blues is a hungry business, and it's hard to charge for medicine work. She needs the guitarist to heal her, to play those harmonics that will reknit her being. Rabbit Food moves quickly between the guests and intruders. Rabbit Food heads to the dance.

Rabbit watches turtles and frogs in the butcher's window. Roast ducks hang in a row next to red sausages that smell of star anise. Candied lotus pods, 100 year-old eggs and boxes of huang chi sit in stacks in front of the store next door. Rabbit sneaks some fresh water chestnuts and bounds after his girl. Rabbit likes blues and he likes tea dumplings. Today he will get both. The tourists ebb and eddy.

Resurrections

Rabbit Food drags her fingers through her wavy hair, making it stand like a roofline full of old style TV antennae. She purses her lips. She takes up the pencil again. Rabbit Food rarely sketches her designs first. She's the first to admit that she cannot draw her way out of an idea. She sketches now: hands with eyes, rattlesnakes, sun disks. She is drawn, haunted by images from Cahokia, from the Ohio River valley. She is drawn, she draws. The curving jaws of serpents, the curving fang. She draws. Spider carries the sun. She draws. Warriors transform, clay transforms, the word spins out under soft graphite. Rabbit Food chews her lower lip, fiddles with her pencil. Rabbit Food rotates her sketch several times. This one eye has a strange oblong pupil, stylized, goat-like. She can see the mounds in her mind's eye. Can smell the ozone of lightning strikes. The abandoned exuberance of full-tilt storm soaks into her sketch, the mumble of contented river. Carved conch stalks her through her notions. She circles the images with transparents: trapezoidal, exact. So much harder to respectfully rebirth tradition than to breathe only one's own air. A pretense of the new or a pretense of the old, either is toxic, unhealthy in large doses.

Rabbit walks the great snake mound, takes on a more human form than is usual for him these days. The snake twists under his feet. Used to being a minor thing in someone else's place, Rabbit is made large, is stunned out of his reverie by the things that come to watch him walk. Secrets from all over the world: a spring guardian from Somerset leans against a rock, an elegantly dressed and jeweled river being from Meroe stands, hands raised in respect. He meets the gaze of a snake legged woman with powerful arms and long hair... was she from the Altai? Rabbit had seen her somewhere before. There was a flash of a short, furry-armed being and Rabbit almost calls to it, but he is busy. He has to walk, has to sing. Rabbit finds this memory, often tucked away with other treasures. He remembers their names, he sings and sings and walks. He is huge with hosting other beings, his land a wealth of secrets: forgotten, remembered, carried along with their people and the children of their people. Rabbit mistrusts too much power, usually avoids it. Here in his place and in this moment he calls everything up and his guests sing with him.

Rabbit Food cuts radishes, tears spinach, scoops out watermelon balls. She finds the cobalt and purple bowl and arranges everything carefully. She finds good vinegar, good olive oil. She scatters nasturtiums, borage flowers, rosemary blooms and cashews on top. Rabbit Food sits on the back stairs and eats her salad with rosewood chopsticks. She is greedy for formalities this morning. 8:30 and it's already hot. Late afternoon will be misery, but she probably won't notice, she is being dragged along by a project, and usually can't even remember her name when that happens. It's not a matter of getting an idea, but being got by one. She sucks a bit of watermelon until it's flat. She will eat, bathe, dress in an auspicious color. She will unplug the phones, put a note on the door. She will work. She will probably be absorbed for the whole day. Rabbit Food crunches through a radish. Rabbit Food stands on an edge, preparing to get out of the way of this new thing she is making. Like tending a fire that needs to last all night, she has to prepare a bit. Yellow Bird and his mate make plans in the plum tree. Invisible now that the leaves have fully come out. Maybe she'll flip some rocks for them before it gets too hot.

Under the old fountain basin Rabbit finds a local salamander. She is grey and brown, lungless, four-toed. She turns her stunning eyes to Rabbit and waits. These west coast beings confuse him still. He can't tell if she's a symbol or a simple salamander. They both wait, her skill set better suited to waiting. Rabbit is known to be twitchy, impatient. He can't take it any longer and does a flip for her. She angles her head to watch him better. She readjusts herself. Arranges her body in a spiral. She rests her chin on her tail and watches. Rabbit cannot resist the audience. Rabbit dances, sings, does acrobatics. Rabbit is the original one-bunny circus. Rabbit performs. Salamander watches; huge wet eyes taking it all in. He finds her strangely elegant, strangely compelling. She draws out of him the weakness in his strengths. She is this wet patch of dirt, this small urban habitat. She watches, neither excited nor bored. Salamander watches and Rabbit frantically performs for her.

Rabbit Food takes a lunch break. She stretches, wiggles her fingers, twists in her chair. 1pm and she's overdue for some kind of change of position. She looks at her work. Frogs cluster thickly on the surface. Picked out in close greens and browns they are persuasive, they are interspersed with those disturbing hands with eyes. Rabbit Food shivers. She won't miss this piece when it's finished. We read Poe and Kafka because they had such disturbing nightmares, but Rabbit Food's work is usually more like eating Kanuti. There is nothing wrong with wanting to remind people of joy. This might be joyful too, but it's a draining sort of joy. Rabbit Food feels a bit empty, that post-blood test weakness is nothing to it. She knows that there are berries and sour apples downstairs. She takes one more moment to contemplate this strange piece. Her grandma would have had a story to go with these images. She knows that she couldn't save all of the old stories, packing for travel it's always hard to know what you will need. She'd had to pick and choose. Half a century away from a full understanding of this particular lesson, she stares at it. She and her brother used to catch penny frogs near Cow Pond. Somehow she thinks that this is not about anything so pastoral. Lunch, after lunch there would be more time to worry about what she was making.

Rabbit grooms his paws until they shine. He cleanses, rubs newly clean paws over his face. Sings a song of clean and happy rabbits. He sparkles, he gleams, he squeaks. Light moves over him like a caress. He basks. He brushes. He chews. Rabbit fluffs his fur. Rabbit is perfect, is beautiful, is purified.

Legends

Rabbit Considers Different Spiders

Rabbit Food dreams of the woman with the finger bone skirt. The fingers gesture and twitch as they talk together of simple, daily things. She morphs, becomes a Thinker. Rabbit Food is chased through the forest by something unseen but horrible. She crashes through branches and comes to an open field where food is set out on wooden tables. An elderly woman pours oil on a pot of boiling water, a man in fancy regalia pokes at a calf's liver. Her gran fans fancy cards out in a complicated lay. She takes a step, nearly falls, and wakes up with a start. 'It's probably not the best of all ideas to eat your mythology whole, particularly before bed', she thinks. She is the only human person in the house; the cat and bird stir sullenly as she flicks on the kitchen light. She is in search of tea, in search of a calming ritual she supposes. Habits or rituals: the comfort food of the mind or thumb sucking for adults. Sleep is so fugitive a thing in her middle age.

A different spider is weaving something in Rabbit Food's garden. Rabbit watches and wonders where HIS spider has gone. This strange spider, male spider, random weaver, sets lines across a span of nearly ten feet. His guy lines and connections look able to catch a small mammal: perhaps a cat or... Rabbit's eyes narrow. There is something about this creature that is familiar, unsettling. The spider turns three eyes on Rabbit and Rabbit remembers. With so many cousins it could be hard to keep track, no one could fault him.

He offers this cousin/spider a dried apricot... offers some crisp basil. Spider declines the offers. Rabbit is flustered by this visit as he is not when visiting certain other tricksters. They are both of them out of place here in San Francisco. Spider keeps weaving. He weaves true and solid, even if erratic-looking. Rabbit smells the crackle of ball lightening. He feels his fur rising. He can see St. Elmo's fire gathering on the tips of tree branches, on parts of this strange spider being. Rabbit feels the magic gather. He becomes uneasy.

The rosemary and fog howl at one another. Rabbit Food makes soup. She washes towels. She strings beads on thread, stitches them down onto deer hide. There are days and days that pull her into herself and pry her out again. It's a kind of tide, or clock maybe. Then sometimes it's as if her beads were cut free of a finished piece and put back on thread in some other order, some other way either without image or with a different image. She wonders if it's wrong that she finds the new order as beautiful, if strange. Rabbit Food spins and spins. She feels on the edge of something wonderful, something awesome in the old sense of the word. She feels as she did just before she learned to read. Some new thing is opening up, opening with a slow and aching pleasure laced with confusion. Chestnut Man's voice anchors her through the phone lines. His low voice speaks of the beauty of words, of wood shaped and sanded. He tells her weather. He tells her people and places. She doesn't know what love is all the time, but she knows longing. She wants to stand in the same light as her man, she wants to keep this terrifying change out of his house, out of his kitchen. She wants his strong back and arms to help her. She needs to be together and alone. Rabbit Food thinks that she needs another cup of tea.

Fox stands on the beach and noses a tar ball. He can feel things suffering for miles in all directions. There is darkness lowered over this place that even his perception can't fathom. This goes deep and high and wide and drifts on wind and water and sand. If Fox were given to horror he would know another name for this. He is not the only thing to come to this place today. He could feel them, all of them. Turtle spirits and mangrove singers: there are things along this coast today that haven't been heard singing for hundreds of years. A thing that even Fox couldn't conjure a name for, a thing from before fur, throws back his head and brings a song of dawn things, a song of being brave in the dark, of the impulse to drag a body out of the water. One by one each of them opens a song, a dance. One by one they weigh in again, overseers of things extinct, of things on the edges and of things that are still strong. One by one they remind each other of what each has been through to get here. They sing a song that cannot be silenced by disinterest or greed. They have come to sing.

Rabbit Food is in no mood. She sits in the quiet, in the basement and mixes paint. She lays butcher paper on the concrete. She rinses brushes. She takes a deep breath. On her right there are shelves full of jam and apple butter. On her left cabinets full of art supplied. She has finished her homework. Rabbit Food takes a brushful of red paint, another of white and a third of a tiny bit of blue. Rabbit Food makes disks of color. She brushes, breathes, dances color. She mixes the tempera very wet. Loves to see the paper dimple. Loves the domed thicknesses when they dry. Even still, like beach rocks, her disks are better wet, better with the heal of creation still clinging to them. She learns them, like a different calligraphy, a different vocabulary. Rabbit Food crushes a bay laurel leaf, she paints the color of the smell. She paints as though there is no such thing as aging, as if there is only color forever. There is only pigment and brushes and water and a surface.

Rabbit falls in love for the fifteenth time today. He contemplates the shape of his new light of life. The battered sweater rests in a cardboard box in the recycle pile. He dives onto it. He rolls around on it. Rabbit finds the texture a revelation. Rabbit falls over and over. Later it may be peaches. Earlier it was new light over the raven tree. Just now his whole being belongs to the softness of this sweater.

Botany and Obsession

The exhalation of some night flower soaks into the walls and floor. It's probably jasmine. Rabbit Food can taste it, like a very fine tea. She listens to the Jasmine. She can feel transformations taking place: in her work, in her body. Everything is always changing. There is no telling where this change is leading. This jasmine, this smell of heading into summer, this flower of bright, sharp heat, this flower scent draws her into its arms and rocks her. She is soothed even as the sight of her beading panics her. She doesn't remember designing, or even beading this shading here, that gesture there. The animals stare at her from the bag. They look at her, through her. She doesn't remember through the spasm of creation that handed her these creatures of glass and thread on deerskin. She shivers with it all. The work takes over more and more every day. These abstractions seem to seep from her sometimes, seem to gush from her at others. She feels the slow drain, can watch herself then. These staring eyes are something else. These whiskers, feathers and scales are something else entirely.

Rabbit contemplates his girl, not his girl anymore he supposes. She is grown deeper, has to work at the silliness he breathes into her. He reminds the flowers in the garden that she needs them, reminds them that they are medicine. He blows into their open blooms, soft and soft. This is a delicate seduction; she is so fragile at these moments. All humans seem disturbed when they are taken by beauty, shaken by the throat they seem to understand. Beauty is mystery, is time travel, is a kind of disturbing magic. Rabbit finds himself wishing that her man were here to hold her down, to hold her to ground, to let the electricity out. The world needs connections, crossings: now more than ever. Rabbit Food, in the arrogance of humanity, believes that it's her changing. Realistically it is everything. Her egotism stops short of the mark, binocular vision perspective invested in, but not believed. She is trembling with changes in the universe, her testing tools unequal to the task and also all that she needs to solve the puzzle. That funny, tall man of hers would help clear things up: would pull her from this absorbing meditation, this dangerous song she is learning. Rabbit feels an unfamiliar concern for this woman. Rabbit blows softly onto open flowers. Rabbit plots.

Rabbit Food refolds the Mylar blanket she carries in her purse. She checks the safety matches in their waterproof container. She opens and checks her vial of anti-venom in the snakebite kit. Her pocketknife, space pen and waterproof notebook are equally examined. Child of multiple cultures, of Tsalagi and Polish and fantasy and sci-fi, she knows that around any corner there may be a paradigm shift. Rabbit Food, all 4'10" and 12 years of her, is prepared. Story in every form offers a map to the universe. She will be prepared if stuck in an alternate reality. She slings her purse back over her shoulder and marches down 24th street. She window-shops, wonders what else she might need in her survival kit. Passing one store she notices chocolate pudding and sour cherry jellybeans on offer. Food, that is what is missing. She goes in, gets a small white paper bag full of sweets. She virtuously and carefully closes the bag and slips it into her purse. Then she thinks, perhaps she should test them now, to make sure of their nutritive properties. Perhaps just one cherry bean...

Rabbit approves his girl's preparedness. He slips sideways through reality often, sometimes not even noticing the change. When is he now? Sometimes he can only tell by the relative tallness of his girl, although later that is less useful. He closes his eyes and breathes deep. It's light out. It's spring again. Rabbit has no clue. He hums, dances a song of whimsy and preparedness in equal measure. He dances the taste of cherry candy. He dances the wisdom of snake bite kits. That toy might have saved him a good deal of fuss in other moments. Rabbit dances change and change, overlap and vanishment. Rabbit gnaws on the toes of a too-serious woman at the health food store. Rabbit alters the reflection of the woman wondering about her smile lines. Rabbit watches his girl eat red red candy. Her lips and tongue go red. Her teeth are outlined in red. Her fingertips get slightly red as well. Rabbit steals one and is not impressed by the taste. Cherries are so much better. Being a creature of trick and pleasure he can only approve of her impulse though. He is imagining a peanut butter and honey sandwich, a helping of Kanuti or even ripe yellow plums. Yes, July plums: Rabbit steps through time.

Rabbit Food watches the park sprinkler as it waters the pathway, the bark of two trees. The water runs away from the roots onto yet another pathway, into a dip in the bare space between trees. She wonders why it is that the watering system cannot be set in a way that nourishes the plants. She watches the mud hole slowly drain onto one corner of a baseball diamond. She watches people flee the water as it comes back around onto the pathway. A red and emerald hummingbird dives through the stream in what, were he human, would be easily identified as exuberance. Two barn swallows join him in aerial acrobatics. Probably this display is something to do with area dominance. Probably they are all competing in some avian contest of will and daring that mere simians would not understand. Probably there is a weighty subtext that Rabbit Food, being so mammal identified, cannot decode. Sunlight pours over the edge of the stand of cypress across the field. It sets fire to the reflective hummingbird. White and black feathers on the swallows spring into a contrast that is almost painful. Sunlight is shredded by droplets of water that cling to tree bark, Rabbit Food now sees why the sprinkler is positioned as it is. Rabbit Food is dazzled.

Rabbit lazes in the sunlight on the very top of the Bank of America building in San Francisco. The building is vulgar perhaps. It may be of questionable wisdom to build so high in a tectonically active area. Still, rabbit likes the moxie of such buildings. He likes their insane overuse of all types of resource but taste. He loves to see them blazing in the night, lights required so that planes don't blunder into them. Rabbit stretches. Rabbit becomes a fuzzy puddle on concrete. His eyes half close and he imagines other good basking zones. He contemplates the London pickle. Do they know that it doesn't actually look like a pickle? Rabbit has never seen a silver pickle. He rolls over and slips into a heat-induced doze.

About the Author

Kim Shuck is a writer, weaver, bead artist and walker on the crests of hills. Her artwork has shown on four continents and her poetry has been published on three. Shuck's first juried publication was in the En'owken Journal out of Canada. Her first solo book of poetry, Smuggling Cherokee, was published by Greenfield Review Press and won the Diane Decorah award from the Native Writers' Circle of the Americas. She lives in San Francisco with grown children, rescue cats and a disagreeable parrot called Bond. Rumors of resident ghosts, demi-gods or well kept secrets cannot be verified at this time.

CPSIA information can be obtained
at www.ICGtesting.com
Printed in the USA
FSOW01n0829110216
16767FS